Tangled Pages
Trinity Elise

Contents

TRIGGER WARNINGS

While this book is at it's core a romance book, there are some very serious topics mentioned in this book that should be brought to your attention before you start to read.

If any of these are a potential trigger for you, please stop reading. Your mental health matters much more to me.

- Emotional and parental physical abuse

- Depictions of violence

- Mental health struggles (anxiety, eating disorders, panic attacks, depression)

- Bullying

- Death/Grief

- Substance Abuse

- Parental Trauma

Because this book contains mature content, it is recommended for mature audiences only, 18+.

TanGLeD PaGes PLaYLIST

When I R.I.P.- Labrinth (Chapter 1)
End of Beginning- DJO
Matilda- Harry Styles
BIRDS OF A FEATHER- Billie Eilish
Moth To A Flame (with The Weeknd)- Swedish House Mafia,
The Weeknd
I Wanna Be Yours- Arctic Monkeys
WILDFLOWER-Billie Eilish
I Love You, I'm Sorry- Gracie Abrams
Cardigan- Taylor Swift
Die For You- The Weeknd
Iris- The Goo Goo Dolls (Chapter 38)
All The Stars (with SZA)- From "Black Panther: The Album"
Look After You- The Fray
Nobody Gets Me- SZA
ceilings- Lizzy McAlpine
Falling- Harry Styles
Shameless- Camila Cabello
Dress- Taylor Swift (Chapter 29)

For everyone who's drowning inside but is brave enough to still have the brightest smile in the room.
Just know that I see you and that I understand you.
This book is for you.

1
Serenity

I didn't want her to die.

I wished she did more times than I want to admit. The last time I wished death on my sister, it came true. And now here I am almost a year after her death at a stupid birthday party in Alix Elizabeth Evan's heavenly honor.

The modern sorority house of Iota Zeta Nu stood tall and proud as the biggest house on Sorority Row at Green Haven University. Before my sister died, this was her sorority. And now her "sisters" were celebrating her life and birthday the only way they knew how: a crazy college party. My lip turns up in disgust as I stand in front of the house watching drunken freshmen make out with more than sober seniors, and the smell of alcohol fills my nostrils tenfold. I drag my feet as I make my way into the crowded party, trying my hardest not to bump into anyone; the last thing my 5'0" self needs is to be trampled by a 6'2" drunken basketball player. God, I hate parties like this.

The crowd of random people dancing in the living room erupt into a synchronous howl as the intro to Labrinth's "When I R.I.P." blares through the speakers. The lights go dark, and the purple strobe lights appear. How fitting. I feel like I'm in a bad Euphoria episode. I roll my eyes and continue my way through the crowd, trying my best to find a quiet place while I wait for Luke to show up and entertain me since I was forced to come here. My eyes widen as I see the huge kitchen through its closed glass doors, with not a soul in sight. Perfect.

I slip into the uninhabited kitchen and let out a long exhale, thankful that I had gotten away from the craziness of the party. I walk over to the white quartz kitchen island and sat down at one of the three highchairs. I run a hand through my curly brown hair as I pull my phone out and see a text from Luke.

> **Lucas:** Serenity Elora Evans you better be at Iota Zeta or so help me God, I will tell every emotionally unavailable frat guy at the party you're DTF.

> You wouldn't dare, Lucas. BTW, where the hell are you?

> **L:** Oh, great! I don't have to go through on my threat, I can tell you're already there if you're looking for me I'm running a bit behind since Ryan decided to change his outfit a million times. Also, stop calling me by my government name, damn it!

> Hurry up, I'm sitting in the kitchen like a loner. Tell Ryan he looks beautiful in anything he wears lol. And I'll stop calling you Lucas when you stop calling me Serenity Elora

L: Lol, we'll be there in like 20 minutes. Wow, so you'll tell my boyfriend he's beautiful but not your own best friend? The shade. But Serenity Elora is such a pretty name, Ren is a boyish nickname, blah.

Thank God, hurry lol. And I always tell you you're beautiful, you drama queen. Ren is a perfect nickname, you hater

L: Whatever, Ren lol. I have to drive now since Ryan needs to touch up his eyeliner or else, we'll be even later to the party see you in a few boo!

I chuckle at Luke's last text and shake my head at his dramatics throughout our entire conversation. My smile stays as I hear the muffled playing of "Dance, Dance" by Fall Out Boy. My head moves to the beat, followed by my humming. I close my eyes, feeling the music, when I hear someone clear their throat, sending me into a minute-long coughing fit as I choke on my spit. When I finally catch my breath, I open my eyes and search for the source of surprise. My breathing feels restricted again as I find those forest green eyes staring at me from across the counter. He leans against the now closed refrigerator with a beer in his left hand. As he brings the beer to his lips, a smirk appears on his lips, liking the reaction I have to the surprise appearance.

His Adam's apple bobs up and down as he swallows the gulp of beer he took.

"What's wrong, Serenity? Not happy to see me?" He moves forward in calculated steps like a cat on the prowl, looking for its prey. His muscled arms flex as he leans on the kitchen island, staring into my soul with that same mischievous gleam in his eyes. His wavy dark black hair sweeps across his forehead like he had spent hours perfecting the perfect curly fringe, which I know from years of knowing this man, it only took him ten minutes tops. His veiny hand reaches out towards my own, and I withdraw quickly, feeling like I was going to spontaneously burst into flames at his touch.

"Can you please not touch me, Ayden?" I drop my hands into my lap, and my fingers pull at the long sleeve of my green GHU Huskies hoodie, the color contrasting with Ayden's eyes. He notices the action, his eyes going back and forth between the hoodie and my eyes; the realization sparks in his eyes as he reads over the last name printed in bold letters splayed across my chest:

ZANDER

"Oh, I see you're still wearing my hoodie." Ayden's hand reaches out towards me again, his fingers lightly gripping the hoodie's drawstring, playing with it. I move my hand slowly and place it on top of his as light as a feather. Ayden's gaze shifts to our hands, and it lifts steadily back up to me. As I hold his gaze, I increase the pressure of my hold on his hand until his eyes switch from calm to panic in a matter of seconds. His thick, neatly trimmed eyebrows furrow as he tries to snatch his hand away from me, but I'm not releasing my grip until he learns his

4

lesson. I lean forward, now over the counter; Ayden and I's faces so close together, his breath fans over my lips.

"I already told you not to touch me, Ayden. I mean what I say, unlike you." I bring my face closer to Ayden's, making my lips ghost over his, and our noses grazed one another.

Serves you right, asshole.

My nostrils flare as I get a whiff of what used to be my favorite smell on this god-forsaken earth: Spearmint. I swear he always smells like spearmint, and it drives me off a cliff to my inevitable insanity. I felt him suck in a breath at our proximity before I put the nail in the coffin that is his heart.

"I guess Alix's bitchiness rubbed off on me before she died. Someone had to take over the role of Queen Bitch, so who better than her own flesh and blood?" As we hold each other's gaze, I see the change in Ayden's. His jaw tightens as his lips draw back in a snarl. The look on his face will forever be imprinted in my brain, and I'll remember it even in my last thoughts when I leave this god-forsaken earth. He finally plucks his hand away from me and steps away in disgust. "What's wrong, Ayden? Are you mad I'm talking shit about your precious ex-girlfriend?" My tone is taunting—and the look in those green eyes that aims towards me is murderous. He lets out the breath he had been holding in, his chest heaving as he grips his side of the counter in a tight hold.

"You are the vilest person I have ever had the displeasure of knowing. Your sister just died almost a year ago, and you're happy you finally have the balls to talk crap about her. Where was this energy when she was alive? Oh, that's right, you were too much of a scared little lap dog to say anything to her face." Ayden takes in a breath so deep and releases it fast—his chest moving in and out rapidly at his labored breathing.

Sometimes it feels like I'm the only one to bring him to the brink of insanity, and I love it; hopefully, it's his karma for breaking my heart into a million little pieces.

Despite finding joy in royally pissing Ayden off, his words cut deep, and I can feel the inevitable tears start to sting in the back of my eyes, but I have to find a way to mask it. I gulp, my throat feeling tighter and more constricted as I blink away my incoming tears. "I have plenty of balls," I scoff at his lame insult, raising my fingers to air-quote the word balls. "Also, I was never a scared lap dog. Alix made my life a living hell the last couple of years by constantly ridiculing me and poking fun at something I couldn't control. Don't be mad that I finally found my voice after she silenced it my whole life."

"Oh, please, she made your life a living hell by teasing you about your skin conditions? And Alix never silenced your voice; you did that all on your own by being a chronic people-pleaser. Do everyone a favor and grow up, Serenity." Ayden rounds the counter and tries to invade my space once again, but I jump off the chair to avoid any more unwanted contact with this man, physical or social. I hate large crowds like this one, but at least I will be away from him.

I take a half step before I feel his strong hand on my forearm like a weight, halting my escape. My arm jerks in his hold, but his grip never wavers in my attempt to get the hell away from him. *What the hell does this sociopath want?*

"Really, Ren? I thought you were stronger than this. Why are you trying to run from the truth before I see the fake tears coming out of those disturbing brown eyes?"

"My eyes are honey brown, asshole."

"Does it look like I give a damn what shade of brown your eyes are, Serenity?" The hand holding my arm flexes as his free hand reaches up to my face and wipes away the lone tear that has made its way onto my cheek. My body feels stiff before my hand decides to move on its own and connects with Ayden's cheek. The loud echo of the slap invades the brief quietness between us. Ayden's head falls to the left at the impact of my slap. He turns his face back towards mine with a sinister grin on his full lips.

My face feels on fire, almost as if I was the one who was slapped instead. As I avert my eyes at the aggressiveness of the stare that his disturbing eyes hold, Ayden's hand trails down to my chin, gripping it with his forefinger and thumb; the pad of his thumb dangerously close to caressing my bottom lip. God, I hate this man; even his fingers felt smooth. His grip tightens on my chin, forcing me to look up at him. His expression makes my stomach instantly flip, the nausea hitting me like a truck. He brings his face closer to mine as if that were even possible, our lips so close, his ghosting over mine. If I move even the slightest, we would be kissing, and that would make this complete nightmare a lot scarier.

"I know you like the position we're in right now, Serenity, considering you were practically in love with me when we were younger, but I'm only this close to you to make my words clear. The next time you try to use your sister to hurt me, I will not hesitate to make your life a living hell. I cared about your sister and even you at one point in my life, but that's over now. You are not special. You are nothing but an empty shell of a person I once knew. I suggest you stay with your pathetic two friends and the bookstore you so dearly love before I do something that I regret."

For a while, I forgot that he knew about my old feelings towards him, and I feel the bile climb its way up my throat, Ayden's words burning like acid. His fingers are currently exploring my face, ghosting over the shape of my lips and cupid's bow; Ayden's eyes following along like I was his favorite movie—except with every second I feel his eyes on my skin, the hatred follows shortly behind.

"You idolized me when we were younger, and I played into it. I loved it—it was a great ego booster. But I don't need it now, and I don't need you, so for the love of God, stay away from me, Serenity." We finally meet each other's gaze and hold it for what feels like forever. His hands are now on both sides of my face, holding it in place, my skin burning at the contact. Even though I feel numb everywhere except where Ayden was touching me, tears escape my eyes, betraying the trust I had in myself to mask my true feelings about the hurtful words poured out to me.

"I don't want to be a part of your pathetic life, Ayden. You stopped being a person I cared about long before my sister died.

Within the last ten minutes of this lovely conversation, you've degraded me and made me feel like the dirt on the bottom of your shoe, worse than Alix did when she was alive. It's nice to know she left behind someone who knows how to break my soul down to nothing just like she did." As his green eyes search mine, I swear I see a flash of hurt in them. Ayden opens his mouth to say something—more than likely even more cruel than the last but we're interrupted by the sound of the glass doors of the kitchen creaking open. Both of our heads turn at the sound, making our lips brush against one another briefly. Because we're so close, I feel his body shiver before he pulls away from me, putting a slight distance between us.

"Everything okay here?" My best friend's penetrating voice rings through the kitchen.

"Yes, everything's fine, Lukas." Ayden's flat tone directs to Luke, though I can feel his eyes burning a hole through the side of my face, probably wishing immediate combustion on me.

"It's Luke, and I wasn't talking to you, Devil's spawn." Luke rolls his eyes as he makes his way towards me. He opens his mouth to ask me again if I'm okay, but I stop him. I just want to get away from Ayden as quickly as possible. I grab his hand and walk to the glass doors, where Ryan is standing, grabbing his hand as well. I turn around to find Ayden with his beer back in his hand, leaning on the island counter, his piercing green eyes hook right on me. I force a bright smile on my lips and shout, "Let's go have a drink for Alix!" as I turn around and pull my friends into the crowded party, leaving Ayden behind, hopefully for good.

***

You know the feeling of being in the present moment, knowing you made a terrible decision, and still making said decision? That is my exact feeling as this random senior has his hands wrapped around me as we're dancing to the beat of Camila Cabello's "Shameless". The party has grown even more crowded than when I first arrived, and I'm shocked I allowed myself to be in this position, considering I hate crowds and generally dislike the opposite sex for multiple reasons, but give me a couple of shots of tequila, and I'm a completely different person.

My hands snake around the stranger's neck, and my body moves in ways I didn't know they could against him, along with the beat. His hands find their home on my lower back, danger-ously close to my ass. He's a couple of inches taller than me, so I look over his shoulder and find my best friends dancing with each other and staring at me with wide eyes and silly grins. My eyes roll as Ryan gives me a thumbs-up and Luke yells through the crowd, "Let's go bitch!" at the same time. Thankfully, the music is loud enough to hide my embarrassment at my friends' antics. It's been a while since I've been at a party like this, and honestly, it feels good. *Or maybe it's the alcohol talking.*

I flip around, turning my back on my supportive and goofy best friends to enjoy the moment of dancing with a stranger and the tequila flowing through my veins, giving me the confidence that is usually nonexistent in me. I close my eyes, feeling the music, and bring my arms back to his neck, grinding my back against his front, his hands dangerously low on my hips. My movements almost halt when I feel his head dip and his warm lips plant a kiss on my now exposed shoulder. Damn it, I knew I shouldn't have worn this tube top. If Ayden hadn't pissed me off so badly, I wouldn't have taken off his hoodie and thrown it in Luke's car the second we had walked away from the kitchen.

Speak of the damn devil. I open my eyes, and the first thing that I see is *him*. He's leaning against the wall, beer in hand, dancing with a leggy blonde girl who has on a red dress so short that if she bends over in the slightest, everyone will know the color of her underwear—if she's wearing any to begin with. Before I have the chance to blink, those green eyes found mine, almost as if he could sense me like I could him.

Unfortunately, he continues to hold my stare, not backing down anytime soon. The blonde girl starts grabbing at his neck and lightly touching his face, desperately trying to regain his attention. He ignores her impressively; his eyes are not connected to mine, but still in my direction. My lips lift into a smirk, thinking our little staring contest was over, and I had won. It's almost laughable how wrong I am.

My smirk drops the second my eyes flip back up to Ayden's face. I thought the look on his face earlier in the kitchen was intense, but Jesus Christ, nothing compares to the look on his sculpted face right now. His jaw looks tense and set in place; there are only two words to describe the look in his eyes: pure chaos

11

and all-consuming fire. And it's directed right at the hands on my waist. My body feels on fire under his intense gaze, and I can't handle it for a second longer. I flip back around to face the stranger I've been dancing against and finally decide to look at him. He is overwhelmingly good-looking; curly blonde hair, light blue eyes, a light scruffy beard decorating his jawline, and quite literally the most perfect set of lips I've seen; minus he who shall not be named, who's currently throwing daggers at the back of my head.

His eyebrow lifts as he shoots me an amused look, bending down to my height, his warm hand moving my wild curly hair out of the way, giving him easy access to talk in my ear. "You danced on me like that and didn't know what I looked like? I don't know whether to be honored or yell at you for dancing with me like that. I could've been a bloody psychopath or something!" My ears perk up at the use of the word "bloody" and the slight Australian accent mixed with an American accent, creating the most interesting sound I've heard in a while.

"Why would you yell at me? We're strangers. Also, if you were a psychopath, you would've already tried isolating me instead of giving me time and reasons to run away from you in a crowded room full of drunken college kids." The nice-looking stranger's full lips hold that same amused grin as he looks me over, his blue eyes shining with mischief.

He leans down to my ear again before he responds in a teasing tone, "First, you still ramble the same way you did when you were five years old; it's a talent, truly. Secondly, if you haven't already gathered, I'm not a stranger, but I'll give that beautiful mind a minute to put the pieces together."

I force myself not to get flustered over that "beautiful mind" line and think about where I know this man from. My brain struggles to process the new information, and for a moment, I'm almost angry that my mind would forget this beautiful creature standing before me. I look over his features again in a glance, and as I see my best friend's face in my peripheral vision, it instantly clicks. A bright smile erupted on my lips.

"Ezra!" I throw my arms around my best friend's older brother. I can hear Luke's laugh over whatever song is playing at the moment. After a couple of seconds, I release Ezra and turn to my left to hit Luke across the back of his head as hard as my dainty hand would allow me.

"Ow, Serenity, what the hell!" Luke cries out as he rubs his hopefully very sore head. Lights suddenly blind us, every light above us in the sorority house turning on. My eyes thankfully adjust to the light quickly, looking for the person who interrupted Ezra and my short-lived reunion, my eyes lingering through the crowd as I take in the sight of everyone adjusting their eyes to the newfound brightness. I finally look straight ahead of me, and my eyes once again connect with Ayden's. He has that same infuriating smirk on his lips, but there's a substitution for the same beer he had in his hand most of the night— it was a microphone. What is he about to do now?

AYDEN

Nothing compares to the sight in front of me. It might be easy to assume that I'm talking about the party we threw in honor of my ex-girlfriend Alix, but no. I'm talking about the look of fury on the most infuriatingly beautiful face belonging to the one woman who haunts my dreams every night I try to erase the memories of her: Serenity Evans. Fate has a sick, twisted sense of humor. Alix's death was the catalyst in all of our lives, but especially Serenity and I's. Growing up, there were moments where Serenity and I grew closer, but I had to make certain decisions that weren't always for my own benefit. I made a vow to stay away from her, but it's like there's always this invisible string that pulls us together. After our heated encounter in the kitchen earlier, I was going to stay far away from her as best as I could—until I saw fucking *Ezra Castellanos* with his hands all over her.

I don't think he knows what he's doing; besides setting me up for an attempted murder charge.

I couldn't care less who Serenity has romantic relationships with. But the one person that she should stay the farthest away from other than myself would be him. So, I decide to take matters into my own hands, knowing the one person that can easily sour Serenity's happy reunion with Elmo—I mean Ezra: Alix. Alix has always been a sore topic for her, even before my ex-girlfriend passed away; their relationship was always tense since my family moved back to Green Haven just before my 10th birthday and my sister Beck's 9th birthday. Beck and I might as well be twins, but we're not; we share the same birthday a year apart.

My memorial speech to Alix was planned for the end of the party, but I ambush Ashley Kent, one of Alix's closest friends and sorority sisters, and work the Ayden Zander charm, as my teammates call it. Within record time, she shuts down the party for me to start my speech, startling the hundreds of drunk GHU students, effectively killing their buzz; Serenity and Elmo included.

I grab the microphone sitting on top of the DJ booth before hopping onto the platform stage set up in the gigantic living room in the middle of Iota Zeta Nu. My fingers tap the microphone as startled college kids look in my direction. The corners of my lips drag up into an amused grin.

I cleared my throat before speaking into the microphone as I scanned the crowd for the only person this was supposed to hurt. "Hey everyone, sorry for interrupting the party, but before things get too crazy, I wanted to make sure to honor the person we're here for: Alix." The crowd erupted in cheers, but I finally found the eyes that looked like swirling pools of chocolate and caramel, and instantly, my gaze penetrates; locked into a trance. "Alix was not only my girlfriend, but she was also so many other great things. She was a great friend, daughter, sister; to all of you at Iota Zeta Nu, but most importantly, she was an amazing sister to her little sister Serenity. In fact, Serenity, why don't you come up and say a few words in honor of your lovely sister?"

If my eyes could somehow produce a hologram of me finally calling checkmate on this game, Serenity and I have been playing all night; they would. Within a matter of seconds, I saw the emotions on her face change; from sadness to shock, back to sadness, then the final emotion that I'm used to seeing from my own 5'0" personal form of hell—pure and all-consuming anger. I saw it flip like a light switch in her eyes.

Before I could damn near blink, Serenity shoved the arm Elmo had wrapped around her waist—goddamn it—oh fuck it, who am I kidding, I don't give a crap what his name is.

Anyways, Serenity marched her tiny feet towards the stage, the anger practically seeping out of her pores. By the time I realized what she was going to do it was too late to stop her. She snatched the microphone from my hand and looked back in disgust as the pictures from the slideshow we prepared finally started showing up on the wall behind us.

Pictures from Serenity and Alix's childhood start to fill the atmosphere, and everyone in the crowd spouts out aws every time a picture of younger Serenity and Alix shows. Serenity's face was a myriad of emotions once again. The next picture that came up in the slideshow was a picture of the day I had met them both. Alix and I were 10, and Serenity and Beck were 8. Alix and I were in the middle, holding hands with Serenity on my side and Beck on Alix's. I smiled as I reminisced about the memory. Serenity's hair was all over the place that day; her unruly dark brown curly hair hit me in the face right after this picture. She had attacked me in a tight hug, and I had returned it, picking her up in the process. Until I had dropped her like she was hot water that had burned me because the heavy winds had moved her wild curls straight into my eye. The only thing I remembered after that was Alix yelling at her, and Serenity ran off into their house with tears flowing down her little puffy cheeks.

Before I have a chance to further go down memory lane, Serenity abruptly turns back to the crowd and decided to finally grace us with her kind words about her sister.

Her hazelnut skin-toned hands gripped the mic so hard; I could see her blue and green veins popping out, threatening to burst at any second in her justified anger towards me. And there it was: suddenly, I understood why girls found veins attractive. But I'll think about that later.

Serenity lets out a strangled, disbelieving chuckle as she shakes her head, her long dark curls flowing from side to side across her back. Her almost bare back: that's only half-way covered by her white crop top, and no longer preoccupied with my last name. My jaw ticks in irritation, but I'm gonna let it slide, assuming she took off my hoodie after our argument in the kitchen. Serenity's stormy eyes locked onto mine before she gave the speech of the century.

"You want me to say a few words on behalf of my sister, Ayden?" She steps away from my side, crossing in front of me to properly address the crowd. "You want me to talk about what an awesome person she was? Fine. I'll do just that." A shiver runs over her body as she inhales in a huge breath, as if she was bracing herself for the biggest moment of her life.

"Alix Evans was the biggest bitch I knew." Gasps collectively fell out of everyone's gaping mouths. Serenity laughed, liking the shocked looks everyone has pointed towards her.

"She made my life a living hell and didn't give a shit. She and her friends bullied me for years, and everyone just stood by and watched it happen." She turned back to me, looking me square in the eyes, her hardened gaze pinning me to the spot. "Including you."

Don't look at me like that. I can't stand it when you look at me like that.

Serenity's puffy cheeks are now glistening from the fresh tears. Her chest is quickly rising and falling, her breathing becoming labored. I can tell the tears are starting to block her vision because she starts to look around, an overwhelming expression spreading across her face. Even though I'm not too fond of her right now, I can't let her do this to herself. Knowing all too well what's about to happen, I try to pull her into my arms and lead her away from the stage, but the second I touch her elbow, her right hand comes flying across my left cheek.

"No, fuck you, Ayden, don't you dare fucking touch me! You knew, you fucking knew you piece of shit!"

Her body thrashes against me as I try to grab her again. Her tiny fists slam into me, trying to do whatever damage they possibly can. I bend my knees and lift her over my shoulder despite her protests. I have to get her the fuck out of here now. I think of an escape plan quickly as I see flashes of cellphone lights from everyone recording the show Serenity just put on. I run off the stage and push my way through the crowd of people recording—Serenity's hits actually making my back ache with the more she throws at me. I nearly double over at the feel of her knee-high boot heel digging into my stomach; my now healed wound slightly opens at the sharpness. My fingers make their way to her lower thigh and pinch; making Serenity yelp and hit me again, but this time with all her strength. Jesus Christ. I finally make my way out of the front door of Iota Zeta Nu and make my way to my most prized possession, my Red 2024 Jeep Wrangler Sahara.

"Fuck you and your stupid soccer mom ass car." Serenity huffs out.

"Such vulgar language from a life-long ankle biter."

"Ankle biter? Fu—"

Serenity's next colorful choice of words is cut off by her friends shouting at us.

"Hey, where the hell are you taking her, Zander?" Luke shouts across the lawn. My eyes roll to the back of my head as I turn back, still holding Serenity hostage on my back as we make it to my car, her head almost smacking against my passenger side door from the movement.

"The one place the spoiled princess can think about how much she embarrassed herself tonight in peace." And with that, I open the door and throw Serenity in the seat, making sure to buckle her in.

By the time I make it to the driver's seat and close my door, she's nearly asleep, but of course, she can't rest until she makes

19

one last snide comment. "I'm not a spoiled princess, but you're definitely the villain in my story, asshole."

"That's fine by me; I'm already the villain in my own story, so why not yours too, Iris?"

"Iris." Her long dark eyelashes sweep across the top of her cheekbones as she lets out a breath, letting me know that she's finally asleep. A rogue curl of hers falls in her face, and my fingers move without thought, tucking it behind her ear softly. As my eyes graze over her, I can't help but notice how the moon illuminates her features. My hand again has a mind of its own because here I am, my hand slowly tracing the outline of her jaw. The realization of what I'm doing sinks in, and I pull myself out of whatever trance I'm in, almost tracing the outline of her lips for the second time tonight. I blow out a rugged, deep breath, turning away from her unsettlingly stunning face, and turn on the ignition to start the twenty-minute ride to Serenity's home.

2
Serenity

Bright light attacks my poor eyes, barely giving me time to adjust. I squeeze my eyes shut as quickly as I can and hide my face in the crook of my elbow. A deep groan escapes past my lips, and I roll over, unfortunately hitting the floor below me. Ow, what the—

I feel around and realize that I landed on the carpet. I move my fingers, feeling around for some clue as to where I am, until I graze a smooth surface that almost feels like a pant-leather shoe. The only person I know in my life that wears pant-leather shoes like they're a religion is—

I force my eyes open and drag them up the legs covered in the brand new Empirio Armani jumpsuit and finally meet the face that is a literal reflection of mine, minus the absolute rage, of course. It's too early for this.

I throw her a sheepish half grin. "Hi, Mom." She is definitely not impressed. Her eyes roll and her upper lip lifts in a disgusted expression, her eyes travelling around the place I call home.

"Get up, Elora," She makes her way to the door of the upstairs apartment of Sunshine Books, kicking the books sprawled across the floor to make a path for herself.

21

"Can you not kick my babies, Mom!" I go into leapfrog position to grab the rest of the books that are in her path of destruction.

"You better be lucky they're the only thing I'm kicking! You have five minutes to come downstairs," Mom calls out from the staircase, and I don't miss the overly sarcastic tone in her voice. I roll onto my back blowing out a deep breath rubbing my face with my hands, wondering how in the fuck my mom found out where I was.

I sit up and expeditiously grab Ayden's GHU hoodie that was on my chair and rush downstairs to meet mom slipping it over my head, making my already horrendous bedhead worse; my curls going in every direction besides one. Ha, get it? One Direction? No? Sheesh tough crowd. I make my way down the weathered dark brown spiral staircase, feeling the bumpy texture of the railing that's been painted over too many times. I should really think about renovating, but I like the old charm of Sunshine Books. I feel my eyes gloss over thinking about the memories I cherish most about this place before I feel every muscle in my body stiffen.

How in the—

Why is my mom, my intelligent but scary mother, sitting down at one of *my* bookstore's café tables drinking a cup of coffee with the devil's spawn himself?

Have I died and gone to hell? The would be the only reasonable explanation as to why I'm seeing him in my bookstore.

"Elora, don't be rude. Say hello to your guests." I drag my eyes away from the devil's spawn and to my mother who still has that same look on her perfectly made-up face.

She lets out a deep sigh, rising from her chair. Making her way towards me, she grabs one of my curls, placing it behind my ear. Her eyes pierce into mine, giving me the look. You know the look; if you're of any Hispanic or African American ethnic descent you know exactly what look I'm talking about. Naomi Evans doesn't play. I pull out of her hold and put a decent amount of distance between us, just in case. Even though I hate his very existence, at least he will be a witness if something happens to me.

"Elora, how many times have your father and I told you that it is not acceptable for you to live here. This place is a damn near a health hazard," her face scrunches up as she once again scans the only place that feels like home with judgmental eyes.

I let out a groan, my fingers weaving into my hair, as I lightly pull at my scalp in frustration. "The only reason why dad doesn't want me to live here is because he has a fucked-up reasoning on why this place should be closed based on his and grandma's relationship."

My mother's hazel eyes narrow at my sudden choice of pro-fanity. I throw up my hands in surrender and continue, "Look, it's easier for me to live here if I'm running the bookstore. Plus, it's closer to campus, so I don't have to look for an apartment when the fall semester starts in a couple of months." If my mom's expression could be more heated, I'd burst into flames on the spot.

"No, your father and I have told you multiple times that you living in that hazard of an apartment was not going to happen and you did it anyway. I understand that you want to find a way to be close to your grandma after all that's happened, but this is unacceptable Serenity. For godsakes, you don't even have reliable security system!"

Letting out a frustrated mini scream, I stomp my feet over to the bat taped underneath the front desk, a cloud of dust hitting me in the face in the process. I cough and wipe the burn of the dust getting into my eyes away, sporting a fake confident expression at my mother.

"See?" I wave the bat around like a crazy person before it slips out of my hand, going straight towards mom's head. Thankfully, she ducks down at just the right second; otherwise, she would have haunted me from the grave for the rest of my life. My hands cover my mouth, my gasp ringing loudly throughout the empty bookstore.

"Mom, I am so so—"

"Enough," she huffs, moving her straightened shoulder-length black hair out of her face, her eyes still closed like she's expecting another object to come her way. When she opens her eyes, she gives Ayden a glance, who, up until this point, I had forgotten was even here. She turns back to me, her eyes softening slightly.

"Ayden told me what happened last night."

"You ass—"

"Hey! Enough Serenity! Shut up when I'm talking and act like I raised you with some manners," I close my mouth with a quickness. Again, Naomi Evans doesn't play. I cross my arms and tilt my head, waiting for her to finish. She glares at me, her eyes tightening and her lips curling into a scowl.

"Get rid of the attitude, Serenity Elora, or I'll get rid of it for you," I have a staring contest with her for exactly five seconds before backing down.

"As I was saying before I was so rudely interrupted, Ayden told me what happened last night at Alix's honorary birthday party. You had missed my calls last night, so when I called you this morning, Ayden picked up your phone and told me what happened. So, I came over as soon as possible."

I finally drag my eyes to Ayden's stupid, smug face. God, I hate him.

"Now, since that explanation is out of the way, back to your dire living situation," Mom starts, but I interrupt her fast.

"I can stay—"

"No, you absolutely cannot stay here, or else I will tell your father."

My blood runs cold through my veins. "Mom, no, please. You can't tell Dad, he'll cut me off and I won't be able to run the bookstore, let alone go to school!" Tears glisten in my eyes, threatening to spill out. This isn't good. Last year, after spring sophomore finals, my mom found out that I had switched my major from pre-med to Writing by GHU, sending our transcripts home by mail. She confronted me about it, and I begged her not to tell my dad. She agreed as long as I kept my grades up and didn't let them slip, in case I got too caught up in the bookstore.

He has never approved of my dream of becoming a published author and running the bookstore. Sunshine Books was his mother's, my grandmother's, bookstore. She ran this bookstore with such love and care until the chemo she had to endure because of her stage 4 Non-Hodgkins Lymphoma.

By then, I took over for her, despite my dad's protests. He wanted me to focus on my pre-med classes during my freshman year and not be distracted by the "fantasy" of books and writing. He always held a resentment against Grandma Shelia and her love for books. Every time I try to ask him about it, he shuts me down and changes the subject.

Mom sighs, rolling her eyes before speaking and switching to her usual stern expression, "Fine, I won't tell your dad, but only under one condition."

In my typical dramatic fashion, I drop to my knees in front of my mom, grabbing the back of her calves in a tight grip. "Please, Mom, I swear I'll do anything." I look up at my mother, and the smile she has sported on her face is just downright creepy.

"I figured you would say that. The only way I won't tell your dad about you breaking our rules and living here anyway is if you go to live with Ayden and Rebekka." I let go of her slowly and rise to my feet. Ayden and I exchange equally mortified glances before we both turn to my mother.

"ABSOLUTELY NOT!"

"THERE'S NO FUCKING WAY!"

We shout at the same time. This woman must be delusional if she thinks I can live with him.

My mother's glare is enough to shut us both up. "First of all, language! Second of all, Serenity Elora Evans, you will live with him and Rebekka, or I'll just have to make a quick phone call to your father..." She trails off, pulling out her phone and typing in dad's number. I reach to grab the phone from her in a rush, but she pulls away at the last second.

"No offense, Mrs. Evans, but I really don't think your daughter and I living together would be beneficial. It would be nearly...c atastrophic."

I turn my head to my left side to meet Ayden's eyes and nod feverishly in agreement. "Totally, Mom I have to agree with Satan's spawn on this one. Absolutely one hundred percent cat-astrophic."

She rolls her hazel-colored eyes at my comment before turning her body to Ayden. "Ayden dear, I love you like you're one of my own; your mother and I are best friends, and I know I can trust you and your sister to look after Serenity. Can you please do me this favor and just take her in?"

She makes it sound like I'm a rescue puppy she found on the street or something, Jesus. I swear, my mother is the most intelligent and conniving person you will ever meet. I'm not even shocked she pulled the 'best friends with your sick mother card' on Ayden. Ayden and Beck's mom has been in a coma for about a year now, but no one really knows what happened. She had been in the hospital sick for a while before Mr. Zander had to put her into the Green Haven Long-Term Care facility.

I turn left to look at Ayden, and to my surprise, I see his usually tough exterior crack. He moves his messy waves of black hair on his forehead back, and he nods at my mother; his forest green eyes shining with unshed tears, the unspoken promise caught in his throat.

In disbelief, I look at my mom, who has the smuggest look on her face. "Well then, it's settled. Serenity, do you want me to send some movers over for your things, or can you and Ayden handle it?"

Can we handle it? I wonder if she can handle her only living child going to jail for murdering her ex-childhood best friend and first love.

What fucking Wattpad romance book did I just fall face-first into?

3
Serenity

I would have begged my mom to not make me move in with Ayden and Beck, but the answer would've stayed the same considering I'm packing the last of my clothes into the trunk of Ayden's soccer mom car—excuse me, Jeep. I feel a gaze burning a hole in my face, and when I look up, it's the devil himself.

As I let go of the suitcase, I was in the middle of arranging to find space between my shoes and books and other piles of books, and I met Ayden's cold gaze. His arms, which are covered in miscellaneous tattoos, are taking full control of my attention because of the white Nike cut-off that is doing wonderful things for the muscles I currently can't tear my eyes away from. "Are you done drooling over my body, or can we get this over with and go to the apartment?"

Ayden's annoyed yet smug face finally comes into my line of vision as I unfocus my gaze on my number one weakness. I roll my eyes at his conceited comment and reach above my head to close the hatch of his trunk with extra force. Ayden's jaw ticks in irritation at the slammed door. "You break it, you pay for it, Evans."

My lips tug into a mocking smile, "Trust me, I'm already paying for it by being forced into your soul-sucking atmosphere, spawn of Satan." Ayden's expression matches mine before he marches my way and grabs my arm before dragging me along with him. When we reach the passenger's side, the hand that isn't wrapped around my elbow opens the door, and he gestures for me to get into the truck. My skin tingles underneath his soft yet firm grip on my elbow, as I imagine burning a hole through his brain at his brief moment of manhandling me.

"Either you get into the car willingly, or I pick you up and put you in there myself, Serenity. You have five seconds," He challenges me before counting down. I am not giving in to his games. I hold his glare, daring him to do it. "One...two...three...four..."

Without warning, Ayden's hands drop to my hips, and he lifts me into the passenger's seat and buckles me in before I have a chance to fight back. My lips part in shock as I let out a gasp at the sudden movement. One of his hands now rests on the headrest next to my head as the other one tugs at my seatbelt, making sure I'm buckled in properly. My cheeks flush at the proximity of our faces, Ayden's spearmint-flavored breath blowing in my direction, taking over my entire sense of smell. His body heat engulfs me, making my own body temperature feel like a hundred degrees.

As he's done checking the safety of my seatbelt, he flashes me a heart-stopping boyish grin, "See that wasn't so bad, was it, Serenity?" He takes a step back and slams my door with the same force that I slammed his trunk with, before walking over to the driver's seat and hopping in. Keeping his eyes ahead and not sparing me another glance, he starts the ignition and, without another word, starts the drive to my new home.

***

My jaw drops as I look at the nicest on-campus apartment complex on Green Haven University's campus in front of me. The tan all-brick exterior building is beautiful with moss and leaves spouting from the cracks. Some of the apartments have balconies attached to the living room, while some don't. Outside, there's a forest green colored ping-pong table with the GHU Huskies logo, underneath a huge Oak tree decorated with giant multi-colored lanterns scattered throughout the branches. My eyes follow the lanterns in awe, barely noticing Ayden grabbing some of my boxes until he walks in front of me. I snap out of my haze before following him.

Jesus, he walks fast. Slow down, you giant, I have tiny legs!

I follow him up the stairs, and we make a left before stopping at the door with a gold label that says 2A. Ayden pushes open the already cracked-open door to the apartment, and once again, my jaw drops in shock. If this is considered student housing, the bookstore apartment I've been living in pales in comparison.

Before I have a chance to look around the spacious apartment, I almost lose my footing at the force of someone's body barreling into mine; arms wrapping around my waist and deep black hair hitting me in the eyes, blocking my vision for the moment.

"The least you could do is hug me back since you've been ignoring my texts for months, Ren." My body softens as I recognize the person glued to me.

Rebekka Zander. Beck. My best friend and the better sibling of the Zander kids. The only person I regret pushing away after Alix died. I wrap my arms around her in a tight embrace as I rest my head on her shoulder. For the first time in twenty-four hours, my body felt relaxed. We stay just how we are until I hear the most irritating sound, his voice.

"If you two are done with this wonderful little reunion, Beck will show you around since I have somewhere to be. I won't be back till ten tonight, so please don't wait up for me worrying your pretty little head off." Ayden rolls his eyes, walking past us and grabbing his keys off the black marble countertop.

"I'll worry if you do come back, that means my dream of you ending up in a ditch won't come true." I throw an innocent smile his way, lifting my hand, waving goodbye.

His jaw is set as he glares at me with full-fledged hatred. "I'm going to ignore that comment, Iris." My eyebrows furrow at the nickname. "Why do you keep calling me Iris?"

Ignoring my question with ease, he turns his attention to Beck. "Make sure you show her everything, okay?"

"Got it. See you later, Ayd." She gives him a mocking salute, earning a playful eye roll from Ayden before he gives me one last look over and walks out the front door to who knows where.

My thumb pointing to where he just was, I ask Beck, "Where is he in a rush to?" She shakes her head and waves her hand dismissively at my question. "Who knows with him, probably just basketball practice and whatever else he does."

My interest peaks at the mention of basketball practice. "I thought the basketball season was over?"

Beck goes around me to the black coffee table, grabs her iced coffee drink, and takes a large sip, not that she needed it; she's a great big ball of energy even without the caffeine. Gulping down the huge mouthful of coffee, she turns to me with a grin so bright I'm almost blinded by the sheer optimism. Grabbing my hand, she takes off in the direction of the long hallway with three doors, each spaced out evenly, giving me a good idea that these rooms are more spacious than they need to be.

I stop myself before I run into the back of Beck since she abruptly stopped in front of the door on the right side closest to the room at the end of the hallway.

"It's time to show you your room, Ren," Beck squeals in excitement.

Maybe living here for three months won't be so bad. The walls were painted a plain white with chestnut brown hardwood floors that looked recently swept and mopped. My eyes follow along the room in awe at the little details that already feel like me. Above the computer desk in the middle of the room, in front of the bed, is a heart-shaped picture collage of my childhood. Pictures with Beck and I, Ayden and me, and all three of us together. There were even a few pictures of me and Alix in there, before it all went to shit. The tears in my eyes are shining just as bright as the fairy lights draped around the room as I spot the little reading nook and bookshelf by the window.

I turn around and find Beck with a proud look on her face. "I decorated it all the second Ayden called me and told me you were moving in with us. I know how much Sunshine Books means to you and how much you love being there, so I—"

I cut her off, leaping into her arms, the force of my hug almost knocking her to the ground like hers did to me minutes ago. "Thank you so much, Beck. You have no idea how much this means to me." I pull back, looking her in the eyes, the weight of my guilt suddenly crushing me. Tears sting in my eyes as I gather the courage to start this much-needed conversation. "I'm so sorry for ignoring your texts, Beck. There has been so much going on after Alix, and then what happened between me and Ayden..." I trail off the memory of that night coming back to haunt me. Beck grabs my shoulders, shaking me softly.

"Rennie, it's okay, I understand. I admit first, I was kind of pissed that you were ignoring me, but I got over it and saw things from your point of view; I wouldn't have wanted to talk to anyone if Ayden died." I inwardly cringe at the thought of Ayden dying. He might be evil, but some part of my heart, a very small, minute part of my heart, still cared about him despite him stomping on mine and shattering it into such tiny pieces that I'm still trying to find a way to fix it before it's too late.

I shake my head in disagreement at the statement. "No, I still should've answered." She rolls her eyes playfully at me before taking another sip of her sugar coffee. My nose scrunches up instantly as I remember exactly how she orders her coffee. "Let me guess: white chocolate mocha with 4 pumps of brown sugar syrup." She flashes me a wide grin, "It's comforting that you still remember!"

I make a fake gagging noise and scrunch up my face, remembering just how bad her coffees usually taste, "You're acting like I could forget! The one time I mixed up your coffee with mine that day in the library on campus, I thought I was going to go into a diabetic coma!" Beck throws her head back, bursting into a fit of laughter, her frantic giggles echoing throughout the room.

"You are so full of shit, Serenity, you know you loved it." Maintaining eye contact with me, she takes another huge gulp of the iced sugar disaster, finishing it in record time. Throwing a wink at me, she turns around, skipping out of the room, humming without a care in the world. I let out a breathy, content sigh following her out of the room and down the hallway back to the living room and kitchen.

Beck is throwing away her empty cup when I walk into the kitchen, taking note of the newer appliances in the college apartment, from the new Nespresso machine to the top-of-the-line smart refrigerator. My eyebrows furrow before asking her, "So, what do a couple of college kids do to get such fancy apartments? I mean, this is really nice." Leaning against the counter in front of me, much similar to how her brother did less than 24 hours ago, those same haunting green orbs burned into me; just attached to the only person who hasn't kicked me while I'm already obviously down.

Tilting her head to the side, she holds her head up, putting her chin on top of her linked hands, threading her fingers together.

"Well, first we got this newly built apartment because father-dearest felt bad he was working so much at the office to talk to us, and secondly, he didn't want us staying in the house of our comatose mom, so there we go." Beck ends the explanation with a ghost of a sad smile on her lips, her usually bright and vibrant eyes now downcast on the counter, trying to find anything to focus on other than meeting my gaze.

I reach across the dark marble counter, grabbing Beck's hand in mine. When our eyes meet, her eyes hold a glossy shine, one that I recognize all too well these days. "I'm sorry, Beck. I can't even begin to understand what you and Ayden have been going through. If you need to talk about anything, I'm here. I know I've been M.I.A. lately, but I'm not going anywhere now. Even though I was forced to live here against my own wishes, I'm glad I was a little bit now because now we can get back to being friends." I smile softly at her, now fresh tears burning at the back of my own eyes. Beck's glassy eyes bore into mine as her smile wavers, her usually optimistic nature cracking.

Walking around the counter, Beck reaches for me, and here we are hugging for the third time in less than thirty minutes. I feel her body shake against me, her cries ringing through the apartment. "It was so scary seeing her like that, Ren. She was so

still, stiff as a board. And Ayden, oh god, I've never seen him so..."
She trails off, the wetness of her tears seeping into my shirt.

"He was so what?" I ask, my curiosity at its highest. Beck pulls
back instantly, sniffling and attempting to wipe her hands dry
with the back of her hands.

"Nothing. Enough about that night; too much sadness. This
was supposed to be a happy reunion, not me dripping snot on
your shoulder." She lets out a breathy laugh, breathing through
her mouth now that her nose is stopped up from the crying and
snot. "It's okay. The only people allowed to cry and get snot on
my favorite One Direction t-shirt are you, Luke, and Ryan." I
giggle, making Beck laugh as well. Our laughter stops briefly as
my phone chimes.

Crap.

"I completely forgot that I have therapy today at 4. My therapist is hosting this new group therapy session every two weeks
that I'm basically being forced to try by my parents and her."
Rolling my eyes, I walk over to the couch and grab my purse,
and opening it, I make sure I have everything. I hear the jingle
of keys before I look up at Beck, who's holding out a brand new
green and white checkered keychain with three color-coded keys
attached to it. Along with the keys is a little open book with a
heart drawn on one of the pages, giving it my own little personal
style.

"The green one is for the front door downstairs to get into the
building, the blue one is for the mailbox, and the orange one is
for our apartment door." I grab the keys from her. "Got it."

"Text me if it runs too late, okay? I don't want to spend all night worrying like a middle-aged mother who just let her sheltered kid go to the Loop for the first time with her friends," she playfully rolls her eyes. I scoff in exasperation.

Crossing my arms, I give her the glare that typically only reserved for her brother. "Really? I am *not* sheltered, thank you very much."

Waving her hand dismissively she says, "Yeah, yeah. Says the girl who always has her nose in a book. Run along to therapy before you're late, Serenity."

I point my finger at her. "You're lucky I like you, Zander."

Her upper lip raises, and she moves her hand in front of her mouth, dramatically making fake vomiting noises and pretending to gag. She stops suddenly, throwing me a blank look. "Save the cheesy, overused nicknames for my brother. I know you still have the hots for him; I don't know why, but you do."

I open my mouth in protest, but my phone alarm rings again. I let out a frustrated half-scream/growl as I stomp to the front door of the apartment. "We'll talk about this later, Becks."

"Unfortunately, we will bestie!" She laughs as I speed walk out the door, slamming the door behind me. As I run down the stairs and make it outside, I look up and notice the clouds have now turned a dark grey, and thunder rings out loudly, making a grand appearance. What great weather to walk five blocks in, to a much-needed, but not wanted, therapy session.

4
Ayden

Your parents shape you into the person you become, more than you think. Growing up, things between our parents were great; they were the typical high school sweethearts, living life the way they wanted, with two kids close in age, and finally moving back to the town that made the very same life they had dreamed of a reality. One day, the dream turned into a nightmare as the magical rose-colored glasses were lifted, revealing the hard and undeniable truth: our life was a lie.

Since that horrible night when my mother fell down the stairs and slipped into a coma, I refuse to talk to my father. *Father*. As if he even deserves that title. A father is supposed to protect and love their family, not hide behind a bottle and practically live in his downtown Chicago office when he refuses to face the truth.

Despite my disdain for Brad Zander—what kind of a name is Brad anyway? It just screams drunk prick frat boy who peaked in high school. Anyway, enough about my piece of shit dad. Days before that night, my mom noticed that I wasn't being myself and decided to make me see a therapist. I protested at first as expected, but once I went to my first session, I realized this doctor is very good at what she does, and her little psychobabble about why I am the way I am is actually very interesting. But the only reason I'm putting up with this every two weeks is because of what I promised both my mother and Alix the night our lives changed forever.

I don't want to end up like him. I can't. I won't.

Which is why I'm sitting in the old rec center staring at all other adults who, like me, have had the shitty cards of life dealt to them while waiting on Dr. Adler to start this new group therapy session, finally. Most of the people here are middle-aged, a few look like they're around my age, and two of them are elderly. A couple of people are running late, so Dr. Adler is giving them extra time to arrive. My leg starts bouncing up and down as the irritation settles into me. Why can't people be on time? I know they don't want to be here any more than I do. My eyes follow each person in the room as I wonder if they're just as ticked off as I am about this meeting starting late. Primarily, the faces of the few elderly people reflected mine, which says a lot about me. Maybe my teammates were right, I do need to get out more. My eyes continue to skim through the rows of people before my throat tightens as they notice one terribly familiar pair of honey brown eyes. Her dripping dark curly hair is a dead giveaway that it's who I think it is. Standing by the doorway, she glances around the room, either looking for a way to escape or a familiar face.

Absolutely not. No way. There's no way.

Out of all the therapists within a 100-mile radius, Serenity and I just had to pick the same one. I'm struggling to form a coherent thought besides the panic bouncing around my brain, while Serenity walks further into the space, oblivious to my presence yet. Turning around, I set my focus on Dr. Adler sitting in front of us.

Clasping her hands together, Dr. Adler stands, commanding our attention, "Alright, everyone, now that almost everyone has shown up, I figured we could get this meeting started." Moving down the middle aisle, she throws a soft smile to the newcomers in the back row, tossing her long blonde and grey streaked hair over her shoulder. She begins to walk back up the aisle, shuffling the index cards in her hands.

"Now I know all of you are here for different circumstances that life has given you, but the main reason why you all are here is because you have one thing in common: you want help. While I recommended that all of you come to these group sessions, it was because I had an idea, one that many psychologists have studied. This therapy group will have a single focus for the next 12 weeks: exposure therapy. This form of therapy is intended to expose you to the things, situations, and even people you fear gradually." My mouth feels like cotton at the thought of being in the same room as my dad. *I need to find a way to get out of this little experiment as soon as possible.*

Shuffling the index cards in her wrinkled hands, she resumes talking. "To make sure these assignments are done in a safe and nurturing environment, I've decided to implement a buddy system—if that's what you would like to call it." Every muscle in my body locks up, the dread creeping up me like a growing weed. In about two seconds, I am going to fall to my knees and pray to

God that Dr. Adler hasn't paired me up with the one girl I can't seem to avoid, no matter how much I try. As she begins to call off the names on the index cards, I slide down the seat, attempting to hide as best as I can.

"And last, we have Ayden Zander and Serenity Evans."

Keeping my eyes focused ahead, I try my hardest not to look around for her. I can already tell without even seeing her that her face is holding a mix of emotions, and I don't have time to focus on how she's feeling when my embarrassment is taking the stage front and center. No one knows I'm in therapy, and I don't want people to know. But the one person I really didn't want to know was her. My head throbs, signaling that a migraine was coming soon. I zone out as Dr. Adler continues talking about the assignments; I don't care because we aren't doing this. I'll find a new therapist before I ever let her into my mind and show her the deepest, darkest parts of myself that even I struggle to avoid.

I feel a hand on my shoulder, bringing me out of my thoughts. I guess I was completely zoned out because half of the rec center basement is now empty except for a few people, Dr. Adler, me, and possibly Serenity, but I can't force myself to turn around and face her right now. Everything feels like I'm going down the highway at a hundred and thirty miles per hour, and I can't find a way to hit the brakes.

Clearing her throat, Dr. Adler carefully sits beside me, examining my facial expressions like a typical shrink. "Ayden dear, are you okay?"

Scoffing and letting out a choked laugh, I turn to her before saying, "No, I'm just sitting here staring at the dust falling in the air for shits and giggles." As much as I need these therapy sessions, there's no way I'm going to get better by being partners with the one person who's at the center of everything. "Dr. Adler, there's no literal way I can be partners with Serenity Evans. I'm sure I've mentioned her to you at least once during one of our sessions, so I'm not sure I understand why you put the two of us together."

Lightly touching my shoulder, Dr. Adler throws an empathetic look my way, her wrinkles and smile lines showing as she gives me the gentlest smile I've experienced from a trusted adult in a year. "Ayden, I know the history between you and Serenity. I typically wouldn't pair up two patients in a situation like this—who share the same trauma in a way—but the more I thought about the pairings, the more it made sense for you two to be put together. While there are many significant differences in what you two went through and are going through, I think the two of you could benefit the most from helping each other face these challenges together." Her words sink into me like a knife. Out of the corner of my eye, I see a blur rush past me, those same dark curls I've seen too much of these last twenty-four hours.

"Just think about it, okay, you need this—you both do." I nod; the promise caught in my throat as I'm too mentally exhausted even to utter the words. Getting up, I give Dr. Adler a tight-lipped smile before walking towards the exit on autopilot. I walk out of the old rec center's front door, the loud creaking of the old and rusted door ringing loudly through the silence. I look down and reach for my pocket to look for my car keys, and when I look up, the very keys almost hit the ground.

"What the fuck, Serenity?" I grab my chest as I almost feel it fall into my ass at this girl scares me half to death, considering she wasn't there a second ago leaning on my Jeep, and there she was, the same irritated look on her face.

She crosses her arms across her chest, making her boobs pop as if they needed to stand out more—the girl was seriously blessed in that department. Forcibly dragging my eyes to her face, she throws me her best glare.

"No, what the fuck to you, Ayden?" she points at me and starts pacing back and forth in front of my driver's side door. "Why are we in the same therapy group? Is this some sick joke you set up? Did you pay Dr. Adler to put me and you as partners? I swear to God, I will gather up all the little upper body strength that I have and punch you in your perfectly symmetrical jaw so hard—"

"Okay, first of all—shut the hell up for once in your life!" I cut her off, making her freeze mid-way into her pacing, her body half turned towards me and the other half to the car door. "I—" Thunder interrupts me, and in an instant, it seems, rain begins again.

"Get in the car."

"Not this again," Serenity throws her head back, letting out an exasperated groan. Raising an eyebrow at her, I extend my hand up and out, challenging her. "By all means, we can stay out in the rain and continue this conversation, but by the looks of it, you already look like a wet poodle, so...," I trail off, putting the ball in her court. Narrowing her eyes at me, she doesn't say anything but stomps against the wet gravel, a puddle splashing my jeans as she willingly goes around to get into the passenger's seat. Fighting the urge to smirk at her finally listening to me for once in her life, I get into my Jeep, turning on the ignition and putting on my seatbelt.

Serenity's eyes widen when she notices me backing out of the parking lot and turning onto the main road. "Where are we going?"

"I think you've asked enough questions today, Iris."

"God forbid a girl wants to know if she's being kidnapped or not."

"Trust me, you do not have to worry about me kidnapping you; you're too much of a damn headache, Iris."

She lets out a low chuckle, shaking her head as she turns to look out the window at the storm brewing in the clouds. "Good to know, Satan's Spawn."

5
Serenity

S taring contests were so much easier when we were kids. Or maybe it depends on the person you're doing them with. As I sit across the booth from him at Poppy's diner, this staring contest is becoming a challenge.

Out of my peripheral vision, I see the diner owner herself, Poppy, appear to take our orders. Breaking the intense eye contact, I greet Poppy with a warm smile. "Poppy! I haven't seen you in so long!" I scoot out of the booth and wrap my arms around the tiny old woman, swaying back and forth in a tight embrace.

"It's nice to see you, sweet pea! We missed seeing you so much. How are ya doing since your sister…" her southern accent cracks at the end at the mention of Alix. Pulling back, I see the fresh tears in her eyes, threatening to spill out. I rock back and forth on my heels, nervousness and sadness creeping into me, making me uncomfortable. "I'm doing okay, Poppy. As best as I can most days." Looking down at my shoes, I feel her worn-down, calloused hand on my cheek, gently caressing me.

"If you need anything, let me know, sweetheart." Poppy looks past me to Ayden. "Ayden, are you ready to order? I'm ready to get you out of here as soon as possible. Tired of seeing that handsome little face every night." She winks at him, his face flushing.

"The fact that you even have to ask me hurts Poppy. Three waffles with a side of eggs, please and thank you." Poppy scribbles down his order and turns back to me.

"I'll take the same too, Poppy." She nods, writing down my order too, before she gives us a big smile and limps away, her curled ginger hair not moving an inch, undoubtedly due to the ridiculous amount of hairspray this adorable old woman uses every day.

I plop back down into my side of the booth, Ayden's eyes trailing my every move.

Taking a sip of my water, I try ignoring the way I feel under his intent gaze. Snapping my eyes back to his, I grow annoyed that we're literally just playing this staring game instead of talking about the obvious. Slamming my cup down on the table, water splashes out onto the table slightly at the force. "Are we just going to stare at each other this whole time, or are we actually going to have a conversation about us being therapy partners?" Ayden's green eyes widen at the last part of my sentence, his shoulders tensing as he quickly looks around, making sure no one around us is listening to what I just said. Leaning forward against the table, his eyes continue to bore into mine.

"Listen, no one can know that I'm in therapy." My eyebrows raise in surprise at his statement. "I have too much riding on this last season of basketball, and it'll be just what I need for the team or my coaches to find out about me being in therapy and think I'm not fit to be captain. We're supposed to be making the captain vote at the end of summer training right before the fall semester starts."

Leaning back against the back of the booth, I tell him, "Okay, fine, I won't tell anyone. My lips are sealed." I mime zipping up my lips and throwing away the key. Ayden rolls his eyes at my theatrics.

"But I have one more question. Why—"

Ayden tsks, interrupting me. "I thought I said no more questions."

"Technically, you said that I ask too many questions, not that I couldn't ask any more. The only way I'm not going to ask any more questions is if I'm dead and gone."

Ayden's lip lifts in a slight smirk. "That can be arranged, Serenity."

Irritation rushes through me. "Like I was asking before I was so rudely interrupted, why are you in therapy?"

His entire body goes rigid, his eyes becoming more distant as each second goes by. He clears his throat before he says, "We don't need to talk about that."

Before I have a chance to try and pull what he's hiding out of him, our food comes to the table. Ayden, in an attempt to avoid answering my next question, begins to dig into his plate. In typical boy fashion, he stuffs his mouth with more than he can chew. I, on the other hand, struggle to put more than a few eggs onto my fork. I look around the diner, pulling one of Ayden's moves, making sure no one is watching me. When I turn back, Ayden once again has his eyes glued on me.

His eyebrows furrow as he looks at me, confused, "What are you looking for? Are you not hungry? You've barely touched your food." His eyes take notice of my barely touched plate as I examine his. He literally has half a waffle left. *What did he do? Inhale it?*

My spine straightens as I sit up, grinding my teeth, "I'm just a slow eater."

Ayden scoffs. "Bullshit, you used to eat faster than me. Your mom and Alix used to call you the 'human vacuum'." He chuckles at the old nickname, but I don't laugh with him.

I nod at his recollection of the embarrassing memory. "Yeah, Alix loved making fun ways to call out my issues and insecurities in front of others, as you already know. But since my trauma is so amusing to you, the reason I haven't touched my food is that I have a phobia. It's called Deipnophobia, and it means I have a form of social anxiety disorder that makes me scared to eat in front of others. Dr. Adler says this phobia might have started after Alix's constant bullying ended up in me in a Psych Facility for trying to starve myself because she was poking fun at my binge-eating disorder. So now, thanks to my lovely sister, I feel like my heart is going to beat out of my chest every time I pick up a fork in the presence of anyone." I raise my hand, gesturing for him to continue. "So please, by all means, go ahead and bring up more memories of my traumatic childhood."

I've never seen Ayden look as distraught as he did in front of me right now. His mouth is parted, shock painted all over his face. "I—Serenity, I didn't—" He stuttered, barely able to get out the words. Holding up my hand, I stop him.

"It's fine, Ayden. There's nothing you can do now."

He looks down at his plate before snapping his head back up to me. "I'm going to find a new psychiatrist."

"Ayden, what? No! You need this to help with whatever it is you're going through, and I for sure need this. Do I necessarily want to be partnered with you? No, but Adler is not changing the assignments, you know she's very strong-minded about this." As much as I wanted to get on my knees and beg Dr. Adler to switch Ayden and me, I knew it wouldn't have worked in the slightest. The woman is college besties with my mom; they're just alike in the worst way: stubborn as hell.

Ayden opens his mouth to argue, but is interrupted by the loud chime of the door opening and rowdy hoots and hollers coming from a group of guys coming into Poppy's. Each of them had on the dark moss green color and GHU Huskies basketball jerseys, and spotted Ayden immediately. The tall and goofy blonde, also known as Garrett Everrett, makes it to our booth first, the rest of them following behind and sitting in the booth next to ours.

"Zander! There you are, we were wondering why you missed practice!" Garrett shoves Ayden playfully in the shoulder before turning to me. Looking me up and down, his gaze heats, checking me out.

"And just who is this beautiful young woman?" he leans in closer to me, grabs my hand off the table, lightly brings it to his lips, and places a kiss. An unexpected giggle comes out of me at the action. If my complexion wasn't darker, my cheeks would've been bright red. Even though in the terms of Luke constantly telling me that I "glowed up", I don't think I'll ever be used to male attention after years of wanting attention from the one person who wouldn't give me the time of day.

"I'm Serenity," I smile up at him, straining my neck at how tall he is. He at least had to be 6'5", which is a giant to me. Garrett smiles down at me when I notice a dimple show on his left cheek, and his bright blue eyes focus on me and only me. Still holding my hand, he opens his mouth to ask me something else, but another voice stops him.

"She's also my girlfriend. So, I suggest you get your hand off my girl before I break it and feed it to you for dessert, Everett." For a second, I think I'm hallucinating until I turn my head in the direction from which I heard the voice. And there he was, the same boy I've loved since I was eight, my dead sister's ex-boyfriend, and the most confusing person on the planet, telling his entire basketball team that me and him are dating.

Yeah, I definitely didn't see this plot twist coming.

6
Serenity

Girlfriend.
   Girlfriend.
Girlfriend.

The word is ringing through my head like a loud echo as I stare into space, ignoring the people around us. Ayden's fidgeting in his seat is what breaks the trance.

"Will you stop moving like a god damn gummy worm!" I whisper-shout at him while side glancing his teammates, noticing they're all distracted by Poppy taking their orders. Ayden looks at me in a panic before getting out of his side of the booth and sliding over to mine, his body a little too close for comfort. He does a half scoot towards me, and in return, I do a half scoot away from him. We do this dance for another fifteen seconds until my heart almost falls out of my ass because I've reached the end of the booth and almost fall on said ass. Until Ayden's hand catches my waist, pulling me back flush against him. I try to ignore every toned muscle I can feel underneath his shirt, my face flushing at my loud thoughts.

"Who's moving like a gummy worm now, Evans?" He mocks me, a playful grin plastered on his annoying face. I lightly shove him back, letting him know I need at least a little breathing room. He scoots back a little, but not enough for my liking, considering that our legs are still touching. Leaning down, Ayden stops at my ear and whispers, "I'm only this close because of them. Once Poppy's done taking their order, we'll pay and get out of here. I'll explain everything on the way home, Ren." I find myself nodding along in agreement, even though my brain is not even fully comprehending what just happened.

Poppy comes over and puts the bill on our table, smiling brightly at the two of us. Without thinking, I reach in front of me for the bill, but before I have a chance to lift my hand off the table, Ayden's large one covers mine.

"What exactly do you think you're doing?"

I raise my eyebrows, throwing him a confused glance, looking back and forth between our hands and him, "Um, looking at how much the food was?" He leans into me again, using his free hand to tuck one of my curls behind my ear. My breath hitches, the closeness too much for me. I feel his soft lips against my ear before he whispers, "I think you're forgetting that you're mine for the moment; pretending or not, there's no way in hell you're paying for anything around me."

My heart hammers through my chest, the world suddenly feeling so closed in and small that I have no room to breathe. Before I can reply with something stupid, Poppy saves me once again by putting a styrofoam box down in front of me.

"Have a good rest of your day, you two. Ah, I just knew you two crazy kids were going to end up together someday, such a cute couple!" Poppy rambles before grabbing Ayden's empty plate and our two cups with a knowing smile and a skip in her step.

"How does she already know we're together? I've only been your fake girlfriend for two seconds!" I whisper-shout at the arrogant man-child who's sporting his signature obnoxious smirk.

He lets out a breathy laugh; my stomach tightens at the sound, the butterflies roaming free. "I mean, why wouldn't she think we're together? You've had googly eyes for me since you were eight years old."

I scoot back from him again, and this time he actually lets me. I let out a scoff, "I have not had googly eyes for you since I was eight years old, Ayden."

He lets out a small chuckle, shaking his head as he gathers my leftovers into the takeout box. It irritates me that he obviously doesn't believe me, but it's also ridiculous on my part because I don't even believe myself when I just said that sentence. It wasn't true; not at all.

Ayden scoots to the other end of the booth with my takeout box in his right hand and stands up. Holding out his left to me, he says, "Are you ready to go home, or are you just going to stare at me all day? You're not really giving me a reason to believe you aren't all googly-eyed over me, Serenity Elora."

"You are insufferable." I huff, grabbing my leftover box full of waffles and eggs, and getting up to go to Ayden's just as equally insufferable Jeep. As I walk past the rest of Green Haven's varsity basketball team, I catch Garrett's eye, flashing him an overly flirtatious smile and waving. His cheeks are flaming red as he turns and focuses his gaze on his plate of food, avoiding my eye contact impressively. I smirk and stifle a laugh as I walk out of Poppy's diner, feeling Ayden's glare burning into the back of my head.

7

Ayden

S weat drips down my face as I finish my last set of barbell rows, the weight slamming loudly on the Green Haven University gym floor, making my teammates look at me in concern. Lifting my t-shirt, I wipe the sweat that's nearly falling into my eyes, my chest heaving at the intense workout. A rough hand slaps against my shoulder, and without looking at him, I can already tell who it is.

"A.J., you good bro? Or have you been too distracted by that sexy little thing you the guys saw you hanging out with last week at Poppy's?" The annoying, irritating voice of my best friend since freshman year makes me see red at his little description of Serenity. Logan Davis is many things, but a man-whore is the biggest. On instinct, my left hand reaches over, shoving Logan so hard he flies into the white brick wall next to us, and the fucker laughs as if I won't beat his ass right here, right now. As he leans against the wall, he runs a hand through his soaked blonde hair, studying me.

"I can't remember the last time you resorted to violence over a girl. She must be throwing it on you good man," He wiggles his eyebrows suggestively. I grit my teeth in annoyance.

"You have one more comment to make about her before I seriously damage your face, pretty boy." This makes Logan smile widely. "Go ahead, I'll have every sorority girl lining up to take care of me—you'll only be getting me more opportunities to get laid."

My lip lifts in disgust. "You have problems, dude, real fucking problems."

Logan lets out a howl, "You're just mad I get more pu—"

"Dude, seriously, shut up."

He holds his hands up in defense. Shaking my head at the idiot I call my best friend, I reach down and grab my workout bag and water bottle off the floor, getting ready to leave the gym since my workout is finished. I roll my eyes at Logan as I walk past, eager to get home and shower after a long day of off-court conditioning. I feel my mood slightly lift as I hit the outside air, the middle of June hot atmosphere instantly giving me a boost of dopamine. As I begin the long walk across campus to my car, I hear annoyingly heavy footsteps following me.

"Wow, so you're just gonna leave me hanging like that? I didn't even know you had a girlfriend, and I've been your best friend for years! I had to find out from Reed and George." Jamie Reed and Blake George were two overambitious freshman power forwards who had somehow made their way onto the varsity team. They're actually pretty good when they're focused on basketball instead of the "Ball Bunnies". Ball Bunnies are what we nicknamed our never-ending "fans" or women who are far more interested in what we have in pants than the game itself. Reed and George are also the biggest gossips on the team. If you want to know the dirt on anyone on the team, you go straight to them.

I abruptly stop in the middle of the quad and turn around towards Logan. "Look, it wasn't planned. It literally just happened yesterday, and I didn't exactly have time to shout it from the rooftops," I explain the situation hastily, trying to end the conversation. Lying to teammates with whom I'm not the closest of friends with is different than lying to Logan. With him, I at least feel slightly guilty. Actually, never mind, I feel awful as I see the dejected look on his face.

"Dude, I'm sorry I didn't tell you, okay? Will it make you feel better if I give that Stacey chick your number?" I offer.

His expression lights up immediately, no hint of sadness present at all. "Why, thank you, kind sir, for your service!" My jaw drops as I realize I just got played.

For the second time in ten minutes, I shove my best friend hard, sending him flying into the soft plushy grass of the GHU quad, the contents of his workout bag spilling out in every which way. My nose wrinkles and my eyebrows shoot up as I stifle a laugh. "Why the fuck do you have condoms in your workout bag? I didn't know you were into guys," As the last sentence leaves my mouth, I can't hold in my laughter any longer. I clutch my stomach, which is hurting something awful right now just looking at Logan's pissed off expression.

"Fuck you, I'm just prepared for anything, you never know when you're gonna need 'em. And even if I were into guys, I would still get laid more than you!" He scowls at me.

"I can't wait to tell Reed and George about your *prepared-ness!*"

"A.J., don't you dare!" Logan pleads desperately.

Laughing, I stick my AirPods in, effectively ending the conversation and continuing my walk to my car.

***

As I toss my workout bag on the floor next to our couch, I plop down on the comfortable dark green modular linen, my muscles finally taking a much-needed break after today's workout. Letting out a deep sigh, my mind wanders to where the girls are; it's way too quiet in here for a Thursday night. I reach into my pocket and grab my phone.

> Dearest sister, where are you?

> BECKS: Where else? I'm prepping for my show.

> Well, I forgot, jeez. No need to get snippy, gremlin

> BECKS: I'm not getting snippy. But now I will if you call me another gremlin, jerkface.

> Oh, calm down Ms. Drama major

> BECKS: Never. If I'm not dramatic 90% of the day, I'll melt away like the Wicked Witch of the West!

> You know she doesn't really mel—you know what, never mind. Hey, where's Ren? I don't think she's here. It's as quiet as a mouse in here.

BECKS: Ren? Whoa, you actually can say her name☒ Usually, you let out weird grunts like you're constipated whenever I bring her up.

> Answer the god damn question, Rebecka.

BECKS: God, okay, no need to get your hormonal panties in a twist! She's spending the night at her parents' house.

And at that last text from Beck, I go into my contacts and call Serenity.

Serenity

"Is there somewhere more important you need to be, Serenity?" My father's stern voice cuts through the silence of the most awkward dinner I've been unfortunate enough to experience in my life. I look up from my plate of mixed greens and sauteed Cod to see my father's blue eyes glaring at me and dart down to my phone, which currently won't stop blinking from the number of notifications I've been getting for the past ten minutes. I throw my father a sheepish grin, trying to lighten the mood, but failing miserably.

"Answer it in the living room before I throw it out, it's giving me a damn headache."

I nod before reaching for my phone, scrambling into the living room, away from the tense environment. My chest heaves as I feel the weight of being in the same room as him being lifted. I turn my phone over, looking over the notifications that were still coming in. Ayden. Ayden. Ayden. *Ayden.* All thirty-five text messages, ten missed calls, and three voicemails were from him. Worry riddles my body, assuming that the worst has happened. I can't lose someone else. *Please, let everyone be alive and okay.* I almost drop my phone, my hands shaking fiercely. I tap my foot as I press call, and thankfully, I don't have to wait long, because he picks up on the second ring.

"Why the hell are you at your parents' house?" He seethes through the phone.

"Excuse me? I'm not your pet. I can come and go as I please, thank you very much." Who does he think he is? Before I have a chance to add more, he catches me by surprise.

"You're right, I'm sorry. What I meant to say was, 'What the hell are you doing at your parents' house without me? That place and they are obviously a trigger for you, considering what Alix did to you, so I should've been there with you." He lets out a huff, needing a deep breath after that bullshit he just spewed out.

"Okay, first of all," I look around to make sure my parents are still in the living room and aren't eavesdropping on my conversation. "Just because we're therapy partners doesn't mean I need you. This is just a dinner, and I'm staying over for the night, so I don't have to have one of them drop me back home."

Home. The word almost feels foreign coming out of my mouth when referring to the apartment as my "home".

Over the last week, Beck and I have fully rekindled our friendship with nightly marathons of The Vampire Diaries and vanilla waffle-cone ice cream. While she has made me feel completely welcome and at home, I haven't seen or heard from Ayden at all this past week, until tonight. My brain is already hurting from this conversation.

I rub my temple, trying desperately to free myself of this headache. "I'll come and pick you up." His tone was definitive, leaving no room for argument. The one thing I can say about Ayden is that once he sets his mind on something, getting him to give up is next to impossible.

My throat feels tight at the thought of Ayden actually coming here. Dad is already looking for reasons to chew me out; I don't need another one. "No, Ayden! Really, I'm fine. There's no need, I'm fine with staying here tonight."

The sound of the front door of our apartment slamming rings loudly in the background on his end. Mere seconds later, I hear the lock of his car chirp and another door slamming.

"Ayden James Zander, don't you dare—"

I don't finish my sentence, because I'm greeted by the lovely sound of three short beeps, and Ayden is no longer on the phone: currently making his way to my childhood home.

***

I have never had such a strong desire for God to send down a lightning strike and take me out of here until this very moment. Finally forcing my eyes away from my plate, I lock eyes with Mom, who I can also tell felt the energy shift from bad to worse the second Ayden sat down at the dining room table, as she averts her gaze to my father, gauging his reaction. She shifts her gaze towards Ayden and me, her eyes holding a curious expression as she looks back and forth between us.

Dad clears his throat, and all the attention in the room goes to him—his glare newly focused on Ayden. I take a deep gulp of my water—hoping to choke and put myself out of my misery immediately. Dad never truly liked Ayden, despite him being Mom's high school best friend's son, and our next-door neighbor since they moved back here to Green Haven. He tolerated him until the day he and Alix started dating when they were fifteen. Ever since, the most Ayden got from him was a glare and the occasional snarky comment. But the night Alix died, they almost fought in the Emergency Room, and as far as I knew, they haven't been in the same room since. I was too consumed by my grief at the time to even pay attention to what they were arguing about, but now I'm curious.

"So," He says finally, setting down his wine glass. "What brings you here, Ayden? Here to date my other daughter?"

Ayden's jaw flexes, but his voice remains steady. "Actually, no. I came here to pick her up and take her home. Didn't want you or Mrs. Evans to go out of your way to drive her back to our place, so I figured I'd do the nice thing for once," Ayden stabs a piece of asparagus from his plate and bites into it, never breaking eye contact with Dad—almost daring him to question him.

Dad chuckles, humorlessly. "How thoughtful." He swirls his wine lazily, eyes still fixated on Ayden, his glare lethal and ready to attack. "I specifically told you to stay away from this family after what you did to Alix. And now my youngest daughter is living under the same roof as you." Dad leans on the table with his elbows on either side of him, before he delivers the fatal blow. "I don't trust you, boy. Your father and I might be business partners, but don't mistake that for affection. My wife might tolerate you. Serenity might think she's forgiven you. But me?" His lips twist. "Don't expect open arms just because you and my daughter stopped whatever feud you had."

Mom's face scrunches in disgust at her husband's cruel words. "George—"

"Mom, don't." The words leave my mouth before I have the chance to stop them. Dad's eyes snap to mine, his glare sharper than ever. My throat tightens. The same suffocating weight I've carried my whole life starts pressing down—the pressure to be enough, to defend myself, to stay silent. I nervously grip the side of my chair, the numbness prickling through my fingers. Then, suddenly, something brushes against my hand beneath the table. Warm, steady, grounding. *Ayden.* I don't look at him, but his message is clear: *You're not alone.*

I inhale a deep breath before turning my attention back to my father. His blue eyes still hold that intense glare, but now for the first time, I see something much colder than disappointment there. *Hatred*. My father has always been critical of my choices—of me as a person in general. Nothing I have ever done was good enough for him, but anything Alix did was perfect. I grew up in my sister's shadow, and now I still can't escape it even after she's dead and gone. My father holds my gaze, daring me to say something.

"Is there something you want to say, Serenity?" He challenges, his voice dripping in sarcasm. "If you want to defend the person responsible for your sister's death, go right ahead."

The room tilts. Mom's fork clatters against her plate. My heart thuds painfully against my ribs.

"Dad," I say, my voice trembling but rising with each word, "Ayden is not responsible for Alix's accident. He was with us at the hospital that night. You *know* that."

He flashes a look of annoyance at me. "Are you really that stupid? I should've known you weren't that smart to begin with after spending all that time with your grandmother in that god-awful *bookstore*," he spat out the word "bookstore" like it was the most disgusting thing he had ever spoken in his life. He balls his hand into a fist, slamming it down onto the table, making the plates and glasses shake by the intensity of the force. "You're just like her, just as oblivious and dull-witted as ever. Maybe if you pulled your head out of those silly books you read, you could see the facts spread out in front of you. He—"

"Enough!" Ayden's opposite hand slams against the table; this time, making Dad's wine glass fall to the floor, shattering everywhere —much like the way my heart did just seconds ago, listening to the way my dad talked about me. My eyes sting as I fight back the fresh tears threatening to spill out. I can practically feel the anger seeping out of him as I look away from my dad to him; his face matches the emotion perfectly. His eyes are damn near into slits, and his jaw is clenched so hard I'm scared he's going to break a tooth or something.

"You can say whatever the fuck you want about me—insult me, belittle me; I don't care. But what I won't do is sit here and let you criticize and ridicule your own daughter—your *only* living daughter—because of what happened between me and Alix that night. I cared about Alix and never wished her any harm, even though my actions that night might've shown otherwise. So be a man and take that anger out on me, not your fucking daughter, asshole." Ayden's words struck a nerve deep in my father; I wouldn't be surprised if he jumped across the table and punched him in the face. But he stays seated, his jaw ticking and the anger simmering in him. His burning eyes never move from Ayden.

"Get out."

Ayden throws a snide smile at him before backing his chair away from the table. I feel a tug on the hand signaling for me to get up. His grip on my hand is so tight I don't think he's ever letting it go. I follow Ayden's actions and stand up, moving next to him. Before we even have a chance of making it out of the dining room door, my father's voice stops me in my tracks. "Think about what you're doing, Serenity. I would hate to close Sunshine Books because of the company you decided to keep."

My body feels stiff and cold, as if a massive bucket of ice water had been poured over me, giving me the dose of reality I so desperately needed. This is who he is. The person who's supposed to protect me no matter what.

For years, I tried to adjust my wants and needs to fit into the perfect bubble he wanted, but I never gave up on Sunshine Books, and he *hated* me for it. He hated his own *mother* for it. But I'm done letting him make me feel like there's something wrong with having a creative spirit. Which is exactly why I ignore the shell of a person who resembles my father and let Ayden pull me along with him to leave the place that no longer feels like home.

8
Serenity

The door clicks behind us, and the quiet is the most peaceful thing I've experienced in three hours. No more clinking silverware, no carefully measured breaths, no invisible weight pressing on my chest from my father's ridiculous standards. Just the soft hum of the fridge and the sound of rain smearing the streetlights into watercolor through the balcony glass.

I take off my boots, and they thunk against the mat. Beck isn't home, thank god. I take a deep inhale. Spearmint. Of course. I swallow a groan.

Ayden tosses his keys I the ceramic bowl on top of the living room table and plops down on the couch without looking at me. I take a seat on the same sofa, but on the opposite end. We don't look at each other or speak; both of us are too mentally drained to do anything. My thoughts on the disaster that happened tonight are interrupted by my phone buzzing back-to-back with notifications. My group chat with Ryan and Luke is the first one that pops up.

> Luke: You okay? I have a feeling that dinner didn't go as planned.

Ryan: Do you want us to come and pick you up?

I toss my phone on the table in front of me and make my way to the kitchen island, stopping to take a deep breath. "Don't," I say before he can even try to say something positive like 'It wasn't that bad,' when that was a literal Category 5 hurricane served with wine and asparagus.

I turn back towards him just in time to see him scrub a hand over his face. The tattoos on his forearm flex, and I hate the way my stomach flips. Traitor.

"I wasn't going to say it wasn't that bad."

"Oh, so you were going to say it was worse?" I climb up onto one of the island's barstools and drop my face into my hands, wishing I could disappear. "Because that would be honesty for once."

His head snaps toward me—green eyes, glassy, dangerous. "You want honesty? Your father looked at me like he wanted to break his wine glass and shove it in my throat. Then he looked at you like you were a case file he couldn't close."

The laugh that spills out of me is sharp and not the least part humorous. "That's called Friday."

"Serenity," he says, softer.

"Like I said, don't." I pick at the side of the barstool. He exhales and moves to the opposite side of the counter in front of me, leaning his hip against it, arms crossed, which only makes his shoulder broader, highlighting every hidden muscle. Rude. "So are we finally going to talk about the elephant in the room?" I'm eager to wrap up the whole fake-dating conversation.

Ayden pauses, and I can see the gears turning in his head; that Captain brain is cataloging every play. Clean lines and no mess.

"Say it," I tell him. "Say whatever strategy you cooked up in the car while you drove us here like a maniac in the storm."

His mouth twitches. "I did not drive like a maniac. I'm a very sensible driver." He argues.

"You changed lanes like you were allergic to staying in one." I deadpan.

He rolls his eyes, ignoring my comment. "We make it official."

My laugh is tiny. "You mean for everyone else. Not us, this is fake."

His eyes pin me on the spot. "Yeah. Fake. We're fake dating." A shiver runs through me as the words latch onto my soul like a threat and a promise.

I let out a shaky breath. "If we do this," I say, "We do it my way. With rules."

He lets out a husky laugh, like he expected me to have rules at the ready. "Okay. Hit me, Evans."

I point at him, "Don't tempt me." I lift my fingers and prepare to count. "Rule one: no kissing."

I see something flicker in his expression—disappointment? Relief? —and it's gone. "Fine, Serenity."

"Rule two: no...touching unless necessary in public. Hand-holding is acceptable, so whatever. But don't put your hands on me when you're itching to make your point." His jaw flexes, the memory catches up to both of us—the kitchen. The stage. The way we know exactly where to press to make the other break. "Understood," he says, nodding.

"Three: we need full transparency where we use the lie. If you need to use it with your team, you tell me before you spring it on me in public," I lift a brow. "No more temper tantrums with your teammates."

He rolls his eyes at my last sentence. "Fair," he grumbles.

"Four: we keep therapy separate from all of this." The words lodge in my throat. "Whatever Dr. Adler wants us to do as partners, we do it, but we don't let this..." I gesture between us. "affect it."

"I wouldn't." his deep voice is quiet. For a second, I see the boy I've known for most of my life—the one who stayed with me in Sunshine Books when I didn't want to go home to Alix's relentless bullying, the boy who got me my first special edition of The Great Gatsby and read it to me every night in the bookstore until I fell asleep. The one who rejected me on numerous occasions, even the ones he still doesn't know that I know about.

My eyes hold his, hoping he can feel my seriousness before I speak. "Five," I finish, "We don't fall in love."

His eyes close. The silence after those words is a living thing, crawling up the walls. "Serenity," he says, and I wish he wouldn't. "We're good at rules. We're not so good at lines."

"Then maybe rules are the only chance we have."

He nods slowly. "Okay. Rules." He pushes off the counter with that same hip and holds out his hand to me to seal the deal. For a wild second, I imagine lacing my fingers through his, like it means something that it doesn't. Instead, I slap my palm against his; firm and quick, businesslike. The contact burns up my arm, and I yank back too fast.

I clear my throat. "Great. We should...do a soft launch."

He looks at me blankly, slowly blinking. "A what now?"

I laugh hard at his obliviousness about the modern social media term. "You know, social media. Nothing too obvious. ...we don't deny if someone asks us, but we don't announce it loudly to the world until we're ready." I stand up and walk back over to the living room table and grab my phone, waving it back and forth. "Luke can help with that."

"God help us all," Ayden mutters, with a ghost of a smile lingering.

Before I can call Luke, the front door jiggles, and Beck breezes in with the storm clinging to her hair like glitter. She takes one glance over us, clocking the distance between us, the tension like a tripwire between our bodies, and plasters on a bright smile. "So how was hell?"

"Hot," I say.

"That's an understatement," Ayden counteroffers.

She drops her keys, belly flops onto the couch, and props her chin on her fists. "And we're doing this? The fake thing you swore you'd never do? The thing that is a terrible idea and also genius?"

I blink as my head tilts to the side. "Did you bug the apartment?"

She shrugs. "Even in silence, you two are loud. So...?"

I look at him. He looks at me. That invisible string pulls tighter. "Yeah," I say, and it sounds like a surrender.

Beck claps once. "Then you need receipts. A photo. Nothing too obvious, just vibes." She hops up and off the couch, snatching my phone. "Come on, you menaces."

"Beck," Ayden warns.

She ignores him, shooing us toward the balcony door where the rain makes downtown Green Haven look in soft focus. "Okay, stand closer. Closer." She grimaces. "Okay, not that close unless you want to break the internet."

I swallow as I step further into his space. Heat engulfs my chest. His shoulder brushes against mine like an accident, and every nerve in my body goes electric. He's careful, too careful, as his hand finds the small of my back in the most PR-safe way possible. Beck's eyes sharply zone in on the action—noticing how even careful feels combustible. She clears her throat.

"Look at each other," she says softly, like it's not the meanest instruction she's ever given. We follow her directions, and our faces shift, like our muscle memories slotting into place. Somehow, he still has a raindrop attached to his eyelash, and I want to lick it off like a dog in heat—*down girl*.

Beck snaps two photos, three. "Perfect! Soft launch achieved." She's already tapping away on the screen. "Restrict comments. No tags. Minimal chaos."

Ayden scoffs. "Minimal chaos where you're involved? That's bullshit."

Beck sticks out her tongue at him. Beck locks my phone, presses it into my palm, and steps back like she's leaving a room where she's no longer needed. "I'm going to shower and then I'm putting on a terrible movie to fall asleep to. If you two want to keep pretending you don't care about each other, try to keep it down to a dull roar, please and thank you."

"Beck," We simultaneously warn, which only makes her smirk widen as she disappears down the hall to her room. The quiet that I craved returns, but it's changed. It has teeth now.

"Well," Ayden says, "the public's handled."

"Not handled," I say. "Distracted."

He nods. "Right." His gaze slips from me to the hallway Beck disappeared into. "We should set the rest of the terms. What we tell your friends, your parents, my team."

"Luke and Ryan have already texted me multiple times," I say. "I'll tell them...I'll tell them something that makes me want to puke."

His lips lift into a smirk. "They'll love that."

"And your team?"

He rubs his thumb over his temple, like he's trying to get rid of a headache. "I'm pretty sure they all know by now. If they start asking questions, though the Captain vote—" he stops.

"You'll win it," I say, before I can stop myself.

He looks at me, surprised. He averts his gaze to the floor. "I don't deserve it," he mutters honestly. The words seem to cost him something. My chest aches like a bruise.

"Maybe deserving isn't the point. Maybe doing better is." I throw him a reassuring smile.

"Serenity," My name sounds like a prayer he doesn't believe in coming from his lips. "About tonight, with your dad..."

"I don't want to talk about him." I fold my arms around myself. "He'll never forgive me for not being the version of Serenity Elora Evans he drew on a napkin before I was born."

His jaw sets. "He doesn't get to—"

"Doesn't he?" My laugh splinters. "He's very good at it. So are you, at times."

The hurt that flashes in his eyes is almost the same hurt that I'm feeling at this moment. "Yeah, I know."

Silence. The rain softens, a light patter across the glass.

"Rule six," He says suddenly.

"There are only five rules that I made."

"Rule. Six." He repeats stubbornly. I arch my eyebrow, waiting for him to continue. "If either of us wants out, we say the word, and we're done—no collateral damage. We take the hit together."

"And the word?"

A corner of his mouth lifts. "Iris."

I hate the way the nickname sounds rolling off his tongue. "You have got to stop calling me that." He crosses back over to the kitchen and starts making tea. After he adds the water to our electric kettle and turns it on, he turns back to me.

"Rule seven," he says slowly, "We don't lie to each other when we're alone."

"We're literally lying."

"Not right now."

I should make a joke. I should call him Satan's Spawn and break whatever god-forsaken tension this is in two. Instead, I breathe. "Okay, rule seven."

And of course, like two idiots signing their sanity away, we smile at each other like these rules mean something.

9

Ayden

Tonight, I decide to sleep on the couch instead of my room because sleeping comfortably in my own bed feels like a lie I haven't earned. The couch cushions smell like Beck's coconut conditioner and the faint trace of spearmint that I leave behind everywhere. I count backwards from a hundred like Dr. Adler told me to do when I have trouble sleeping. I make it to eighty-five before the shape of Serenity's beautiful mouth drags me under its spell.

Sleep comes like it always does; too heavy and fast, and then it turns on me like a bad habit.

I'm back there. *That* night. Her screams, her voice, the panic rises in my throat mixed with bile. The sound of metal scraping against one another and across the gravel that I will never have the fortune of forgetting. *"Why her, Ayden? Huh? Why Seren—"* and then the gut-wrenching gargle of Alix struggling to breathe, always struggling to breathe. The nightmare always folds into panic before I even realize that I'm awake.

My chest is like a fist that I can't unclench. The air is gone, and my body doesn't know how to breathe. This is my punishment. I lurch upright, the sweat clinging to my skin like hot wax, but the room is tilting and spinning. I can't see, my vision is blurred, I can't breathe, and I can't *stop*. My heart is trying to punch its way through my ribs, and my hands shake so hard I can't press them to my chest. Every inhale is a sharp pain in my throat. It's almost an out-of-body experience—I can hear myself gasping, choking, but there's not a damn thing I can do.

And then there's a voice.

The room snaps into focus in blurred flashes. Serenity's bare feet on the plush rug. Her hair is in a satin scarf. Her beautiful, honey-brown eyes are wide with terror. She kneels in front of me, close but not touching me, as if she touches me, I'll break.

"Breathe," she says gently. "Just breathe with me, okay?"

"I-can't—" My chest jerks and I bend forward, my head dropping to the front of her shoulder.

"Yes, you can." Her voice stays calm, even though I feel her pulse racing in her throat. "In...and out. Match me, Ayden."

She lifts my head from her shoulder, palms on both sides of my head, her fingers grazing my ears. *"Watch me."*

I do as I'm told and hold her gaze. She exaggerates the action, inhaling slowly and deeply through her nose, then exhaling through her mouth. My attention zeroes in on her mouth, memorizing its movements, burning its finality into my brain. It takes four tries before I can mimic her movements. My breath comes out broken, but *finally* it comes. I cling to the sound of her voice, grounding and real, until the room stops spinning.

"You're okay," she whispers. "You're here. You're safe, Ayden." It's only then that I realize she's holding my hands. At some point during my panic attack, she must've reached for them. Her thumbs move in slow, careful circles over my knuckles. These tiny, but anchoring touches are keeping me tethered to this very real moment in time, not the past. My breath stutters, then steadies again.

"Count with me," she says softly. "Four in, four out."

We do it together. Once, twice, and again. The storm that was outside and found its breeding ground in my chest starts to slow its violent brewing. My heart is still pounding, and the sweat cools on my skin. I blink, and the room is the living room of our apartment—the hum of whatever program I played before bed on the TV, the glow of the streetlights through the curtains, and Serenity's eyes locked on mine.

"I'm sorry," I rasp when I finally trust my lungs to work. "I'm—God, I'm so so—"

She squeezes my hands. "Don't. Don't apologize for this."

I shake my head, shame scraping raw in my throat. "You shouldn't have seen tha—"

"Ayden," her voice is firm this time, enough for me to stop and listen. "You're allowed to break down. You're allowed not to be okay."

Something in my soul cracks at her words. My head drops backwards onto the couch, and she shifts closer, sliding next to me on the couch. She doesn't question me; she sits there, waiting for me to be okay. "Was it a nightmare?" she asks quietly as I lay my head on her shoulder, the exhaustion of what I just went through hitting me hard. I nod once. I don't tell her what the nightmare was about. I don't tell her that I see Alix's face every time I close my eyes. Or that the last words that left her sister's mouth were about her, and questions of why I was finally going to tell Serenity I loved her. The guilt of that last conversation with Alix crawls under my skin and chews at me until I can't breathe every single night. I just nod, because that's all I can do.

Her fingers lace through mine. "Next time," she whispers, "you don't have to go through it alone."

The words gut me. Because I want that; I want her, more than I have any right to. And it terrifies me. "Serenity," my voice breaks around her name. "You should hate me." She leans over and drops her head on top of mine.

"Maybe I do," she whispers. "But right now, I don't."

The silence is louder than any confession I could make. My breathing finally evens out, but my heart is still racing and not from panic, but from how close she is and how good it feels to have her this close to me. We sit like this until the night stops buzzing in my ears and the only thing left between me and sleeping peacefully is the steady rise and fall of our breaths in sync. It's the last thing I hear before sleep finally takes me.

10
Serenity

The first thing I notice as my eyes flutter open is the light leaking through my curtains in my room, and not the living room. The last thing I remember is falling asleep on the couch with Ayden after his panic attack. My heart feels like it's running a marathon at the memory—Ayden gasping for air, his eyes wide with terror. Grasping at anything to anchor himself, and that anything was me. I press the heels of my hands into my eyes and groan into the quiet. *What the hell are we doing*?

I don't know how long I lie in my bed staring into oblivion, but eventually I find the courage to slip out of bed as the smell of coffee and sweet potatoes hits my nostrils. I pad over to my mirror, and my reflection looks as conflicted as I feel, my curls in a messy bun, my skin red from the stress of trying to pull Ayden from the trance he was in. I grab my black hoodie from the back of my desk chair and slip it over my head before walking out of my room and into the kitchen.

I stop abruptly at the sight of his toned back facing me. He's sitting at the kitchen island, elbows on the counter, and head bent like he's been awake for hours. There's an untouched mug of coffee in front of him. His hair is an absolute mess; those dark waves are going in every direction. Suddenly, his head jerks up and turns in my direction, like he could sense me.

"Morning," I mutter.

"Hey." His voice is low and raw. "I made coffee."

"Thanks." I walk over to the cabinet and grab a mug from the lowest shelf. As I go to fill my cup with coffee, I freeze in place, noticing the pan on the stove filled with a familiar dish. I swirl around, my heart pounding as I look at Ayden in awe.

"You made sweet potato hash with kale and egg whites?"

"Well, we both know Beck doesn't even know how to make oatmeal without burning it, so yeah, I made it." He averts his gaze, downplaying that he made my favorite breakfast. I clear my throat and grab a plate from the dish rack, filling the plate before sitting on the barstool a seat away from Ayden. I begin to dig into the dish, and a deep groan almost slips out of my mouth, but I catch it just in time.

The room falls silent, other than the sound of my fork scraping against the plate, and Ayden finally sips on his coffee. Finally, he clears his throat. "I'm... sorry you had to see that."

I set my mug down harder than I mean to. "Don't."

"Serenity—"

"No," I cut in. "You don't get to apologize for that. You didn't choose it."

His jaw tightens, but his eyes don't leave mine. "I did, though. All of it. Every single thing that leads up to nights like that? That was me."

And there it is. That sharp, familiar ache of guilt radiates off him. The same one he hides behind sarcasm and distance and stupid fake-dating schemes. Last night, it was bare and shaking on our living room couch.

"Maybe," I say, quieter now. "But you're still here. You're still fighting through it. That matters."

He exhales, a humorless breath. "You shouldn't have to take care of me."

"And yet," I murmur, fingers tightening around the mug, "I did."

His mouth opens, then closes again. There's a long pause, the kind that stretches between two people who are both afraid to move closer and terrified of walking away. "Did I scare you?" he asks finally, voice barely above a whisper.

I hate that question. I hate the way it sounds like he's bracing for me to say yes — like he *expects* me to leave. "No," I say honestly. "But it scared me that you were alone when it happened before."

He looks away, jaw working. "I usually am."

The admission guts me more than it should. I want to reach across the table and touch him. I want to yell at him for carrying all that weight alone. I want a thousand contradictory things that don't make sense.

Instead, I nod. "Well... you're not now." That gets him to look at me again. And for a heartbeat too long, we sit there, tangled in a silence that isn't hostile, but isn't safe either.

11
Ayden

She's different this morning.

Not softer—Serenity Evans is never soft—but quieter. Like last night stripped something out of her, and she hasn't decided whether she wants it back.

I haven't slept since I woke up from my mini nap in Serenity's arms and put her sleeping body back in her own bed instead of on the couch with me. Every time I closed my eyes, the panic sat just beneath the surface, waiting to drag me under again. And every time I thought about that, I thought about her — kneeling in front of me, voice steady, grounding me when I couldn't do it myself.

No one's ever done that for me before.

I run a hand through my hair and stare down at the table, but I can *feel* her gaze on me, like sunlight I don't deserve. "I have more to explain about last night..." I start, then stop because I don't even know where to begin.

"You don't have to explain," she says quickly.

But I do. "I wasn't... dreaming. Not really. It's not just nightmares."

Her mug pauses halfway to her lips. "Then what is it?"

I swallow, feeling my throat tightens as I try to find the words. "Guilt. It's my reality. It's... everything. Every choice I made, every mistake I made leading up to that night. It just—" I snap my fingers, the sound sharp. "—grabs me and doesn't let go."

Her eyes soften in a way that makes my chest ache. "You're human, Ayden."

"Humans don't ruin multiple lives in one night."

The words hang heavy, and she doesn't argue or question what I mean by multiple lives. She just sits there, staring into her coffee like the answers might be hiding in the steam.

We fall into silence again. The tension isn't explosive — it's quieter, heavier, like gravity. Like the pull between us is stronger now that we've seen each other at our worst.

The scrape of her chair breaks the silence. Serenity stands, moving toward the sink without looking at me, but her shoulders are tight, like she's holding herself together with invisible stitches. I can tell she's trying to keep the morning from tipping into something raw.

"Serenity..." My voice comes out low, rough. I don't even know what I'm asking for. Forgiveness? Understanding? A reason to stay?

She rinses out her mug, sets it on the counter, and finally turns. "You can't keep carrying it like this," she says, almost a whisper. "You're going to drown."

"I already am." I drag a hand over my face, fingers trembling. "Last night wasn't a one-off. It happens every time I close my eyes. And it's always the same—sirens, glass, her struggling to—"

"Stop." She crosses the kitchen in two steps, the scent of her shampoo clinging to her hair. Her fingers hover an inch from my arm, like she wants to touch me but isn't sure if she's allowed. "You don't have to go there."

But the words spill anyway. "I can't stop seeing it. I keep thinking maybe if I stay awake, maybe if I stay close to you, it'll be different." My voice cracks on the last word, and it's humiliating how much it costs me to say it.

Her eyes flicker, soft and bright at once. "Ayden..." she says, and this time she does touch me — fingertips brushing my wrist, steady, grounding. "You don't have to keep punishing yourself."

I don't know who moves first, but suddenly she's closer, her forehead resting against my shoulder, her arms wrapped around my body in a tight embrace. For a second, the panic that's been chewing at my ribs all night eases, replaced by a tremor I can't name.

"I don't know how to be around you without ruining you too," I whisper.

"You won't." Her words are firm, almost fierce. "You're not the only one who gets a choice, and you're not the only one who's already ruined."

The kitchen feels too small for everything unsaid. Then, because I need something solid, something normal to hold onto, I murmur, "There's an open gym for the team this morning."

Her head tilts, studying me like she's weighing every hidden meaning. "You want me to come?"

"Only if you want to." I force a faint smirk, though it feels more like a shield than a joke. "Could use someone there to make sure I don't put my fist through more than a hoop."

Something in her eases, not a smile exactly, but the edge of one. "Then let's go. Maybe you'll finally stop this pity party you threw for yourself."

Her words stick in my chest, heavy and electric all at once. She tosses me the hoodie I left on the couch, the fabric soft and warm as it lands in my lap. "Finish your coffee. We'll leave in ten."

And just like that, the air between us shifts again — weighted with something unsaid, but pulling us forward, straight toward the gym. Straight toward whatever waits there.

12

Serenity

The gym feels like it's humming.

The sound of sneakers on polished wood, the echo of the ball, the crowd's low chatter — it all blends into a kind of heartbeat. It's louder than I expected, and somehow, Ayden is right at the center of it.

He's already on the court when I slide into the bleachers with Luke and Ryan. Luke's grinning, relaxed, while Ryan looks like he's just here for moral support.

"Glad you came," Luke says, elbows on his knees.

"Didn't realize it was optional," I tease.

He smirks. "You could've said no."

"Would you have listened?"

Before he can answer, another voice joins in — smooth, familiar. "Would've been a shame if she had."

I glance up and my stomach drops a little. Ezra.

Luke's brother, all casual confidence and easy smiles.

"Ezra!" Luke stands and gives him a quick handshake. "Told you to come watch — Ayden's been lighting it up lately."

Of course Luke invited him.

Ezra slides into the seat beside his brother, his eyes flicking to me. "Serenity. Didn't expect to see you here."

"Guess we both got dragged into it," I say evenly.

He grins, like we're in on some private joke. "Could be worse company."

Before I can respond, the whistle blows.

Ayden moves like something's chasing him. Sharp, relentless, almost angry. Every drive to the basket feels like he's trying to outrun whatever's inside his head. And every time his gaze flickers toward the bleachers and lands on Ezra — sitting too close, smiling too much — his movements get harder, faster, meaner.

The crowd cheers when he sinks a three-pointer. He doesn't smile. Doesn't even look at his teammates. Just glances up — right at me — before turning away.

"Guy's intense," Ezra mutters beside Luke. "He always play like he's got something to prove?"

Luke laughs. "That's just Ayden."

Ezra leans forward, chin resting on his hand. "Or maybe he's just trying to impress someone." His eyes flick toward me again, blatant.

I feel my pulse in my throat. "You really can't help yourself, can you?"

He grins, unbothered. "Not when it's this fun."

The final whistle shrieks. The scrimmage ends with Ayden's team on top, and the crowd scatters in a wave of voices. Players slap hands, grab water, talk over each other — but Ayden doesn't join them. He heads straight for the bleachers.

And the look on his face stops me cold.

He's still breathing hard, sweat dripping down his temples, eyes locked on Ezra like he could knock him out with just a stare.

Luke stands, smiling. "Good game, man—"

Ayden doesn't answer. His focus shifts to me. "Can we talk?"

The tone isn't a request.

Before I can respond, he reaches out — not rough, but firm — fingers closing gently around my wrist. The heat of his hand shoots straight through me.

"Ayden—"

He doesn't wait. He pulls me with him, down the bleachers and toward the gym doors, cutting through the crowd that parts without a word. My pulse is racing, half from surprise, half from something else entirely.

I glance back once — Ezra's watching, eyebrows raised, half-smirking like he's just confirmed whatever he wanted to know.

Outside, the air hits cool and sharp against my skin. Ayden lets go, running a hand through his damp hair, jaw tight.

"What the hell was that?" I ask.

He doesn't look at me right away. "Didn't like him looking at you like that."

"You mean Ezra?"

"Yeah. *Ezra.*" He finally meets my gaze — eyes dark, voice low. "He shouldn't even be here."

I cross my arms. "Luke invited him. He's family."

"He's a problem."

I exhale, the corner of my mouth twitching upward despite myself. "You're jealous."

He scoffs, but it's weak. "I'm not—"

"Yes, you are."

He steps closer, close enough that I can feel the heat radiating off his skin. "Maybe I am," he admits, quiet but fierce. "I don't like the way he talks to you. Or looks at you. Or the fact that he can, and I can't say anything about it."

For a second, neither of us moves. The sounds of the gym echo faintly through the closed doors behind us — whistles, laughter, sneakers squeaking. But out here, it's just us, breathing hard in the silence.

"You didn't have to drag me out in front of everyone," I say, but it comes out softer than I mean it to.

He looks down, regret flickering through his expression. "I know. I just—couldn't stand it."

I shake my head, trying to fight the smile tugging at my lips. "You're impossible."

He exhales, shoulders dropping. "And you're still here."

And with that, I can't argue.

13

Serenity

The air outside is cool enough to sting.

It smells faintly of rain and asphalt, that late-evening quiet that follows chaos. The sound of the game still hums faintly through the gym doors, but out here, it's just us — Ayden pacing, jaw tight, hands on his hips like he's trying to burn off everything he can't say.

I lean back against the brick wall, arms folded, waiting.

He stops finally, exhaling hard. "I shouldn't have done that."

"Dragged me out?"

He nods once. "Yeah." His voice is low, rough. "I just—when I saw him sitting there, looking at you like that..." He trails off, shaking his head. "It got under my skin."

I study him. His shoulders are still tense, his breathing uneven, but it's not anger anymore. It's something else — fear, maybe. Possession. The ache of someone who's been holding back too long.

"Ezra's just... Ezra," I say finally. "He flirts with everyone."

Ayden's laugh comes out humorless. "That's supposed to make it better?"

"Maybe not," I admit, "but it means it isn't about me."

"Everything's about you," he mutters before he can stop himself. His eyes widen a little, like he wants to take it back — but he doesn't.

And just like that, the air shifts.

I swallow hard. "You can't just say things like that."

"Why not? It's true." He steps closer, slow and deliberate. "You think I don't notice the way you look at me when you think I'm not paying attention? Or how you're the only one who can pull me out of my head when everything's falling apart?"

"Because I care about you," I say quietly.

He stops right in front of me now, close enough that his shadow blends with mine. "And that's exactly why I can't lose my mind every time someone else looks at you. But I do. I can't stop it."

There's something in his voice that hits deeper than jealousy — something raw and scared.

I reach out before I can think twice, resting my hand against his chest. His heart's racing. "You don't get to be jealous of every person who talks to me, Ayden."

"I know." His gaze flicks down to where my hand rests against him. "But I want to be the one who gets to."

The confession lands between us, unsteady and real. I feel my breath catch — because I know exactly what he means. He takes another small step forward, the space between us dissolving. "I didn't mean to pull you out like that. I just—couldn't breathe in there. Not when he was looking at you like..." His voice trails off again.

"Like what?" I ask, even though I already know.

"Like he saw what I see."

For a long moment, neither of us moves. The gym doors creak behind us, a muffled burst of laughter spilling through before they shut again. And then it's quiet—just the sound of our breathing and the hum of the streetlights above.

Finally, I whisper, "You're a mess."

He smiles, small and crooked, the kind that always undoes me. "Yeah. But you're still here."

I sigh, unable to help the faint laugh that slips out. "Unfortunately."

He tilts his head, eyes softening. "You don't mean that."

And he's right. I don't.

Because even with his jealousy, his temper, and his walls — there's something about the way he looks at me like I'm the one thing anchoring him to this world that makes it impossible to walk away.

When he finally reaches up, fingers brushing against my wrist, the touch is hesitant — almost reverent. "I don't know what this is, Serenity," he says quietly. "But I know it's the only thing that feels real right now."

My chest tightens. "Then maybe that's enough."

He nods once, slowly, like he's memorizing every word — and for a while, we just stand there, breathing the same air, letting the rest of the world fade out.

14
Serenity

The next morning starts wrong.

Not catastrophic, just... off. The kind of ache that makes even the air feel too heavy to move through. I know the feeling well — the deep, pulsing burn under my skin that warns me before I even look. Hidradenitis Suppurativa flare. Again.

I bite down a groan as I shift in bed. The movement sends a sharp sting along my armpit. Perfect. I drag myself to the bathroom, flick on the light, and brace against the counter. The mirror confirms it — an angry red boil, tender and swollen. The pain feels like it's in my bones, radiating heat.

I've dealt with worse. I've dealt with this for years. But today, the frustration hits harder — maybe because I'm tired, maybe because last night I had to watch Ayden drag me out of the gym like I was some fragile secret he couldn't handle in public. Maybe because I'm just done pretending I'm unbreakable.

I dab warm water on the flare, trying to be gentle and not cry. Not because of the pain, but because I hate this version of me — the one who's forced to slow down, to rest when I'd rather fight.

The knock on my door makes me freeze.

"Serenity?" It's Ayden. Of course, it's Ayden.

I stare at the door, as if I can will him away. "I'm fine," I lie.

"You don't sound fine."

"I'm not doing this right now." My voice comes out sharper than I mean. But the thought of him seeing me like this — sweaty, hurting, exhausted — twists something ugly inside me. He's seen my strength, my walls. Not this.

"Can I at least—"

"No." The word echoes harder than I intend, and the silence that follows it stretches out like punishment.

I press my palms against the cool counter and breathe through the throbbing pain. I know he's still out there, probably running a hand through his hair, probably trying to figure out what he did wrong.

He didn't do anything wrong. Not really.

It's me. It's my body, my flare, my constant reminder that I can't control everything no matter how much I want to.

When I finally open the door, he's sitting against the wall, legs bent, looking up at me with that worried expression I both crave and resent.

"What happened?" he asks softly.

I shake my head. "It's just... one of those days."

He starts to stand. "Can I help?"

I hesitate. The answer should be no — because help means vulnerability, and vulnerability means letting him see me without the armor. But the way he looks at me — not with pity, but patience — cracks something open.

"Just... sit with me?" I whisper.

He nods, no questions asked, and when he settles beside me on the bed, I rest my head on his shoulder — careful, quiet, but real.

The silence isn't awkward this time. It's steady. Healing.

And for once, I let myself believe that maybe I don't always have to fight alone.

15

Ayden

She's sitting on the edge of the bed, her back straight but her hands clenched in her lap like she's holding herself together piece by piece. I can see it in the way she winces when she tries to put her arm down, in the tiny hiss she tries to swallow.

"Serenity," I murmur, "what's going on?"

She exhales slowly. "It's called Hidradenitis Suppurativa or HS. It's a chronic skin condition. It's one of three skin conditions that Alix made fun of me for throughout the years." She smiles sarcastically. "Basically, my immune system is attacking itself, and I get these fun boils all the time."

The words sound too practiced — like she's said them a hundred times to people who never really understood.

I move off her bed and kneel in front of her. "How bad is it?"

She gives a shaky half-laugh. "Bad enough that I'd rather you not see."

I tilt my head, searching her face. "You don't have to hide from me."

Her jaw tightens, like she wants to argue but can't find the strength. Finally, she sighs and grips her hoodie, slowly taking her left arm out of her sleeve. As she lifts her arm again, I see the edge of a red, irritated boil full of pus in her armpit. It looks painful; swollen and inflamed. My chest tightens at the sight. Not because it's ugly; it isn't, but because she's been walking around carrying that pain in secret.

I keep my voice low. "Does anything help?"

"Warm compresses. Tea tree salve sometimes. Mostly just anti-inflammatory meds and rest."

"Then let me help," I say.

She hesitates again—the same kind of hesitation that comes from years of people making her feel like a burden. But then she nods, just barely. "Okay."

I get up and go into her bathroom looking in her towel basket for a clean rag. I turn on the sink all the way up to get it hot enough for her. After I wring it out, I make my way back to Serenity and kneel in front of her, the steam curling between us. She sits still, tense, as I press the cloth gently against her skin.

Her breath catches and her opposite hand grips her black sheets like it's the only thing keeping her from screaming. "It's okay," she whispers, maybe more to herself than to me.

"Tell me if it's too hot," I say.

She shakes her head. "It's perfect."

We sit there like that — me kneeling in front of her, holding the towel in place, her shoulders slowly unclenching as the warmth sinks in. The silence feels different now. Softer.

When I finally look up, her eyes are glassy. Not from pain — from something else. From trust.

"You know," I say quietly, "you don't always have to be the strong one."

Her lips twitch, a small, tired smile. "And you don't always have to try and fix everything."

"Maybe not," I murmur, "but I can try to make things hurt less."

She lets out a shaky laugh, and I swear something inside me settles.

For the first time in a long time, it feels like I'm doing something right—not by saving her, but by staying.

I keep the cloth in place until the water cools, then replace it, careful and slow. I nudge her, signaling her to scoot further into her bed so she's laying back and comfortable. She scoots to the middle of the bed, laying on her good side, facing me so I can still hold the warm towel against the boil. Her breathing evens out, her eyes flutter closed.

"Better?" I ask, moving one of her curls behind her ear.

She nods, voice barely above a whisper. "Yeah... better."

And I don't move — not until she's asleep, sitting up, head resting lightly against my chest. Because I know that if I do, I might break the one fragile moment where she finally let me in.

16
Serenity

By the time the sunlight stretches across my floor again, the pain has dulled to something I can live with. The flare still burns under my arm, tender and raw, but I've had worse. The physical pain is easy—it's predictable and familiar.

What isn't easy is waking up and seeing Ayden still here.

He's asleep in the chair beside my bed, hoodie rumpled, one arm folded behind his head. There's the towel on the nightstand — the one he used for the boil last night. A small, meaningless thing. But my chest tightens anyway.

He stayed.

And he shouldn't have.

Because this is what Ayden does — he shows up, gets too close, makes me feel something real again...and then disappears like it meant nothing. He did it before. Right after Alix died. And once right before she died. One day he was there—my friend, my anchor—and the next, he was just *gone.* No explanation, no goodbye, just silence.

And I told myself I was done needing him after that.
I told myself I'd never give him another chance to break me.

So why does a part of me want to crawl into his warm strong arms and thank him for staying?

He stirs as I stand, rubbing his eyes, his voice rough with sleep. "Morning."

"Morning." I cross my arms, trying to sound indifferent. "You didn't have to stay."

He blinks at me, confused. "You were in pain. I wanted to make sure you were okay."

"I was fine."

"Serenity, you could barely move last night."

The way he says my name —soft and careful—makes my throat tighten. "I said I'm fine, Ayden."

He frowns, straightening. "You don't have to push me away."

That does it. The wall I've been holding up cracks just enough for the bitterness to spill out.

"Push you away?" I laugh, but there's no humor in it. "You mean the way you pushed me away? When I needed you most?"

He freezes. I can tell he wasn't ready for that.

"After Alix died," I continue, words trembling now, "you just stopped talking to me. One day you were there, and then nothing. No calls. No messages. Just silence. Do you have any idea what that felt like?"

His face shifts the guilt, shame, and regret all morphing into one, but it doesn't matter. The damage was already done.

"Serenity, I—"

"Don't." I shake my head, tears threatening at the edges of my voice. "You don't get to disappear, then come back when it's

102

convenient. You don't get to care when it fits into your life." I throw my blanket on my bed, and turn away from him, my heart hammering in my chest, feeling like it could burst through my skin at any moment. "You even stopped talking to me weeks before her accident, so honestly, I don't even know why I was surprised you did it for a second time."

"I wasn't trying to hurt you," he says quietly. "I thought staying away would help. I thought you'd hate me less if—"

"If you vanished?" I cut in. "If you made me think I didn't matter?"

He swallows hard, eyes flicking away. "I was a mess."

"So was I," I whisper. "The difference is, I didn't do everything in my power to push you away."

The silence stretches, heavy and unfixable.

Finally, I take a step back and point to the door. My voice is steadier than I feel. "Please go, Ayden."

He hesitates, like he wants to argue, but then nods. "Okay."

The door clicks softly behind him, and the sound punches through the air like a goodbye I didn't want to hear again.

For a long time, I just stand there, staring at the empty chair. The mug. The faint dent in the blanket where he sat all night.

And when the first tear slips down my cheek, I hate myself for it.

Because even after everything — even after the silence and the heartbreak — a part of me still wanted him to stay.

17

Ayden

The clang of weights hitting the rack echoes through the empty gym, sharp and hallow. At seven o'clock in the morning, most if not all of the GHU athletes are sleeping off their extracurricular activities from the night before, while I'm fighting for my life to erase the way Serenity looked at me almost a week ago.

Her voice keeps replaying in my head.

"You don't get to care when it fits into your life."

Each word lands like a hit, and I don't know if I'm angry at her or myself deserving it.

I grip the barbell and lift, my arms shaking under the strain, the metal biting deep into my palms. I need the pain. I need something to drown out the noise in my head—the noise that's been there for years.

And just like that, the sound of her voice fades, and another all too familiar one take its place.

My father's.

"You think you're tough now, Ayden?" My father's voice snarled, low and slurred. The unbearable stench of whiskey filled the kitchen, thick enough to choke on.

"Look at you. Useless. You can't even take a punch without crying like a little bitch."

My knuckles were split open from the shear force of the punch that sent me flying into the wall, my hand scraping against the broken glass of the empty tequila bottle dad dropped in his normally drunken state. I remember staring at the floor, my blood smeared on the light wood floor and refusing to cry, even though all I wanted to do was crawl into a ball and cry until I stopped breathing all together.

"Dad, stop," I said. My voice shook almost as violently as my body. It did nothing but make him laugh.

He stepped —close enough for me to feel the heat of his breath when he spoke. "Stop? You don't get to tell me to stop in my house. You're nothing without me. You hear me? Nothing!" He jabbed a finger into my chest with each word, hard enough that I stumbled back by the force. "You can't even protect your mother. See what I'm doing is trying to toughen you up—turn you into a man. You're too soft. Pathetic."

I saw mom's long blonde hair through my peripheral as she slowly approached us. Her entire body shook and the look in her eyes were desperate. "Enough, Brad. Please."

He spun towards her, his face red as fire, eyes wild. "Don't tell me how to raise my son!"

"Raise him?" she spat out. "You're doing nothing but make him your personal punching bag! First it was me, now Ayden, who's next? Rebekka?" The glass hit the wall beside her head before I even realized he'd thrown it. It shattered inches from her head, the remnants of the Whiskey bottle he was drinking in replacement of the tequila he dropped, now decorated her hair and body. She flinched but didn't back down—not until he let go of me and focused in on her.

I quickly moved between them, my arm wrapped around Mom. I looked him in the eyes but all that met me was darkness. The man I once knew as my father died a long time ago; this was something much more menacing, like all of his demons came out to play at once.

He laughed loudly. "What are you gonna do, huh? You think you're man enough to stop me?" He grabbed the arm that was wrapped around Mom forcefully, and twisted it behind my back. All I felt was pure, hot pain as my shoulder felt like it was being pulled out of its socket. I hear him take a step back before his heavy boot collided with my back knocking the wind out of me and me falling face first to the floor.

I tried to stand despite the pain coursing through me, but before I'm even two inches off the ground, his boot landed on me again, this time with much more force. I think that maybe he'll actually put me out of my misery and finally do it. But instead I heard Mom's footsteps and I turned my head just in time to see her move backwards towards the stairs. The hold *his boot had on me immediately lifts as he tried to catch up to her before she got away.*

He stalked toward her, shouting — I don't even remember what. Just the sound. The kind of sound that makes the air split. I yelled for him to stop, but it was like shouting at thunder.

Mom turned and ran up the stairs. He followed.
I still remember the way his boots hit the wood — heavy, uneven, closing in.

"Dad!" I'd screamed, chasing after them.

There was a sharp crash, the sound of wood splintering, then silence.
Too much silence.

When I reached the top of the stairs, she was lying halfway down, motionless. His face had gone pale, all the color draining out as he backed away.

"Mom?" My voice was small. Useless. "Mom!"

Her eyes were half-open, unfocused. The rest is a blur — my shaking hands dialing 911, the sirens, the flashing red lights painting the walls.

She never woke up after that.

I blink hard, dragging myself back to the gym. The smell of sweat and metal replaces the phantom scent of whiskey, but the nausea lingers.

Every time I close my eyes, I see her fall. Every time I think about Serenity, I hear his voice: *You can't even protect your mother.*

I press my forehead to the barbell, breath shuddering. I don't know how to stop the loop — the guilt, the fear, the memory of that night. The same night of Alix accident was the same night my mother went into a coma. I couldn't bare to be around Serenity after Alix died because it felt too close to that kind of loss again. Too much like watching someone slip away while I stood there, frozen.

And now she hates me for it.

Maybe she should.

Because no matter how much I try to lift, to run, to forget — the truth doesn't change:

My father and I both destroyed my mother's and Serenity's lives that night.

I've spent every day since trying to prove to myself I'm not like him and I've failed ever since.

18

Serenity

A week.

That's how long it's been since the morning I told Ayden to leave — even though he never really did.

We still live under the same roof. We share the same four walls, the same kitchen, the same silence that sits between us like something physical. It's the kind of quiet that hums—heavy, electric, always threatening to crack.

I've almost gotten used to it. The quiet. The routine. The pretending.

Almost.

I'm sitting on the couch, scrolling aimlessly through my phone, when his name lights up the screen.

Ayden.

For a second, I just stare at it — my thumb hovering above the notification in hesitation. My stomach twists in knots. The last time we spoke, I threw every ounce of anger and frustration I had at him. And now he's texting me like the world hasn't shifted since then.

I open it anyway.

Ayden: Hey. Just wanted to let you know Dr.Adler isn't gonna be in for the rest of the sessions idk if you saw the email.

OMG no I didn't. What happened? Is she okay?

Ayden: She's fine but her father passed away, he had dementia. So she's gonna be away with her family until the end of summer.

Wow, that's so sad So how are we going to do our assignments?

Ayden: You still haven't looked at the email Serenity?

My eyes roll.

Of course not! When have I had time to in the five seconds you just texted me?

Ayden: I don't have time for this. Meet me at O'Malley's at 7.

Someone woke up on the wrong side of the bed today obviously. Wait a minute... staring at his last message it finally hits me: O'Malley's. The campus bar O'Malley's where the entire population of GHU students flock to on the weekends? He must be joking.

I think the protein shakes have finally started to mess with your brain especially if you think I'm

> willingly going to O'Malley's w/you on a friday night

I see the speech bubbles pop up and disappear, waiting on his inevitable response.

> Ayden: Like I said, meet me at O'Malley's at 7 Serenity. I'm in the middle of basketball conditioning, I'll see u later.

> Fine, see u at 7.

I don't bother arguing back with him; it's useless. I might as well start getting ready now to avoid the headache.

By six-thirty, I've changed my outfit three times.
I settle on a black long-sleeved going-out top; fitted, soft, low at the neckline, and tight jeans that make me feel like I have some control over my own body again. It took me damn near three hours to straighten my hair; which is why I usually keep it curly, but tonight is different. It feels strange to care this much about how I look when I know he's seen me at my worst — feverish, crying, shaking from pain.

But still, I care.

I decide to go with my signature makeup look: a little concealer, blush, mascara, and my favorite lip combo; brown lip liner and Fenty lip gloss.

I reach for my phone on my desk and quickly glancing over my reflection in the mirror.

"Shit," I curse underneath my breath. It's seven twenty; I'm late.

I grab my purse and ran out into the living room, stopping dead in my tracks.

Ayden is here on the couch, scrolling away on his phone. Why is he here? I mean, yes, I know he lives here too, but we were supposed to meet at O'Malley's. I guess he senses my presence because his eyes immediately find my black wedges and travel thier way up my body in the most intense gaze that has ever looked upon me. When his eyes finally reach my face, time stops and it's only us two in the universe.

"Wow," he exhales, sitting up straighter. "You—" He shakes his head a little, like he's trying to get rid of and replace whatever he was about to say. "You look...beautiful."

I roll my eyes, brushing off the compliment, even though I can feel my heart practically beating out of my chest. "Can we just get this over with? I'm already late."

"Yeah," he says, standing up. "But you're forgiven at this point."

He looks me up and down again, laughing softly. "If I go to jail and get kicked off the team for kicking somebody's ass tonight blame yourself, Evans."

"Shut up and let's get this over with already," I mutter, shoving past him toward the door, feeling the corners of my lips turn up at the thought of him beating someone up for me. What can I say? I go feral for the 'touch her and die' trope.

19
Serenity

O'Malley's is louder than I remember — a tangle of laughter, clinking glasses, and music thudding through the walls. My nerves buzz with every sound.

Ayden finds us a small table near the back, away from the chaos. The light from the neon sign above catches in his eyes when he looks at me, and I swear he's been smiling since I walked in.

"You look really nice tonight," he says, leaning forward.

I roll my eyes, though my pulse jumps. "You've said that about five times."

He shrugs, still watching me. "You deserve to hear it five more times."

The waitress drops off my food, and I stare at it, my stomach twisting. The thought of eating in front of everyone still knots my insides.

Ayden notices. He always notices.

"Hey," he says softly, nudging the plate a little closer. "You don't have to rush."

"I just—" I stop, exhale slowly. "It feels stupid to be scared of something so small."

"It's not small," he says. "It's brave."

He picks up one of the fries, holds it up between us like a peace offering. "Try it."

I shake my head, but his hand stays there — steady, patient, teasing the faintest smile out of me.

"You're impossible," I mutter.

"Persistent," he corrects.

He moves the fry a little closer, eyes never leaving mine. "Come on, Serenity. Just one."

The sound of my heartbeat drowns out everything else. The air between us thickens — not because of the crowd, but because of him. Because of the way he looks at me like the world's narrowed down to this one tiny act.

I lean forward, close enough to feel his breath, and take the bite from his hand. My lips brush his fingertips.

For a second, neither of us moves.

His jaw tightens almost imperceptibly. He swallows, then lets out a shaky breath that sounds a lot like mine.

"See?" he says softly. "Told you it wasn't so bad."

I lean back, pretending my heart isn't pounding. "You're ridiculous."

"You're blushing," he says, a grin tugging at his mouth.

"Am not."

"You are."

"I'm black, you can't even see me blush." I deadpan, struggling to keep a straight face.

"Stop making perfectly logical debates, woman."

He laughs quietly, and I can't help but join him. The sound between us feels easy, alive, dangerously close to something I remember loving.

When the plate's nearly empty, he rests his chin in his hand, still watching me. "You know, you've got this whole tough-girl act down, but when you let your guard drop, you're kind of..."

"What?" I ask, wary.

He hesitates — just long enough for it to sting — then says, "Unbelievably beautiful."

I shake my head, smiling despite myself. "You really don't know when to quit, do you?"

"Not when it comes to you."

The words hang between us, thick and unspoken and too honest.

I look away first, pretending to check my phone, but my lips betray me with the faintest smile.

And for the rest of the night, the noise of the bar fades into a blur. It's just him, me, and the feeling that maybe this isn't just an assignment anymore — maybe it's the beginning of something neither of us is ready to admit.

20
Serenity

F riday night at Green Haven University is loud enough to hear from the parking lot. Music thunders from the old brick frat house, the one Ayden's teammate Micah swore could "shake the foundations of campus."

I should've said no. Crowds still make my chest tighten, and pretending to be someone's girlfriend for an entire night is the last kind of exposure therapy I need.

After we finished at O'Malley's, Ayden got a call from his teammates about the party. I was going to say no, but Ayden mentioned this would be good practice for us on the fake-dating side of things.

"You ready?" Ayden asks from the doorway. He's in a dark tee and jeans, sleeves rolled, confidence radiating like it's effortless.

"Not even close."

He grins. "Perfect. That'll make the act more believable."

"The *act*?"

"You know—fake dating. People here love rumors. If the more we show them that we're actually together, maybe they'll stop asking questions."

My heart jumps. "And what happens when the rumors don't stop?"

He smirks. "We deal with it later."

The frat house glows with string lights and noise. Micah spots Ayden immediately, pulling him into a handshake-hug while shouting, "My guy!" A crowd gathers, beers in hand.

Ayden slides his arm around my waist, casual but firm. "This is Serenity," he says. "My girl."

My girl.

It sounds too natural coming from him.

I manage a small smile as a few of the guys whistle or tease him, but Ayden's expression doesn't change. His hand stays on me, grounding, steady, protective.

For a while, it's not terrible. The music drowns out my nerves, and people are more interested in talking about the upcoming tournament than watching us. I even laugh once or twice.

Then I see him.

Ezra.

Standing across the room, red Solo cup in hand, smile still dangerous. Luke's brother.

"Didn't think I'd see you here," Ezra says, as he steps closer, running a hand through his blonde curls. "Looking good, Serenity."

I open my mouth, but Ayden beats me to it. His arm tightens around my waist. "She always looks good."

Ezra's eyes flick between us. "So... you two are officially a thing now?"

"Something like that," Ayden says, voice steady but sharp around the edges.

I elbow him lightly. "Relax."

"I *am* relaxed," he mutters, jaw tight.

Ezra laughs, hands raised. "Hey, I didn't mean anything by it."

But Ayden's already tense. I can feel it in the way his muscles coil around my waist, the storm brewing behind his expression.

"Maybe we should get some air," I whisper, trying to diffuse it.

Ezra smirks. "Don't let him scare you off, Serenity. I still owe you a dance."

Ayden turns his head slowly, eyes locking on him. "She's taken."

Before I can react, Ayden's hand slides up to the back of my neck, his touch firm, his gaze locked on mine. For a heartbeat, the whole party blurs—the lights, the noise, everything.

Then he kisses me.

It's not soft. It's purely possessive. It's the kind of kiss that feels like a line drawn in permanent ink, a declaration and a dare all at once. The crowd whoops somewhere in the background, but I barely hear it.

When he pulls back, his breath fans against my lips. "Now he knows," he says panting for air.

I stare at him, my heart pounding. "That was unnecessary."

He swallows, those dangerous green eyes flicking down to my lips, then back up. "Hmm, maybe. But I really don't give a fuck."

Ezra's gone when I glance around again. The room's still spinning, but for a completely different reason now.

I step back just enough to catch my breath. "You can drop the act, Ayden. Point proven."

He nods, but his expression doesn't ease. "Yeah. Sure."

We don't talk for the rest of the night.

But as he starts saying his goodbyes to his team, the anger of him using me to prove a point to Ezra is finally boiling to a head. While he's distracted, I detach his arm from my waist and stomp out of the packed frat house. Immediately I feel him on my heels; I guess he wasn't as distracted as I thought.

21

Ayden

She turns and starts walking down the street, the echo of her heels hitting pavement like gunfire.

Every step she takes away from me feels like a fuse being lit.

"Serenity," I call.

Nothing.

"Serenity!"

Still nothing — just the sharp swing of her hair and the sound of her voice when she snaps back, "Go home, Ayden!"

Something in me snaps.

I catch up in three long strides and grab her arm before she can bolt again. "You're not walking home alone," I bite out. "It's almost midnight, you've been drinking, and this part of campus isn't safe. I'm not letting you walk around by yourself wearing that!"

Her glare could cut glass. "I don't care! Let go of me!"

I shake my head, tightening my hold just enough that she can't yank away. "Not happening."

"I'm not a child. You don't get to decide what I do."

"I'm not trying to decide what you do— I'm trying to keep you safe!"

Her laugh comes out cold and furious. "Oh, please. You don't care about me, you just care about your stupid ego. You think dragging me around makes you the good guy again?"

That one hits deep. My jaw locks, teeth grinding, heat rising in my chest. "You really think I'm doing this for my ego?"

"Yes!" she snaps. "You don't get to kiss me in front of everyone, break the one rule I said I didn't want broken, and then pretend you're protecting me. I don't need saving— especially not from you."

She tries to storm off again, but I move faster this time.

"Fine," I mutter, low and dangerous. "We're doing this the hard way."

Before she can react, I hook an arm around her waist and lift her clean off the ground.

Her breath catches — a startled yelp — and then her fists start pounding against my back. "Put me down! Ayden, I swear to God, if you don't—"

"Keep swinging, Evans," I grunt, adjusting her higher on my shoulder. "You'll tire yourself out before we even reach the car."

She kicks, heel connecting with my thigh. "You're insane!"

"Probably," I mutter, walking faster. Her hair brushes my neck and before I realize I'm doing it, I tilt my head closer to hers and inhale deeply, sniffing her. The scent of her tea tree and honey shampoo and the warmth of her body against mine is enough to drive me insane. Within seconds I can feel my pants tightening. *Fuck. Maybe I am insane.* "But at least I'm not stupid enough to let you wander off into the dark alone."

"You're kidnapping me!" she shouts, her voice half muffled against my back.

"Call it whatever the hell you want," I throw back. "But you're getting in that car."

People outside the frat house are laughing and whistling as I pass, which only makes her squirm more. "Put me down, Ayden! You're embarrassing me!"

"You'll live," I growl, finally reaching the Jeep. I swing the passenger door open and set her down, but before she can bolt, I lean in close, blocking her escape with one arm on the door frame.

Her chest heaves, cheeks flushed, eyes blazing up at me. "Next time," she hisses, "try asking instead of manhandling me."

I lean down, my voice dropping low. "Next time, try listening before you make me lose my mind."

For a heartbeat, neither of us moves. Her lips part, breath shaky, big brown eyes locked on mine — and I can't tell if she's going to slap me or kiss me again.

Then she shoves me, muttering, "You're unbelievable," as she climbs into the seat and slams the door.

"Yeah," I mutter, circling to the driver's side. "So are you."

The engine growls to life, matching the pulse hammering in my chest. She folds her arms, staring stubbornly out the window.

"Don't talk to me," she says flatly.

"Wouldn't dream of it," I answer.

But as we drive through the empty streets, I can still feel the ghost of her against my shoulder — the weight of her, the fire of

122

her anger, and the truth burning under all of it: I'd carry her a thousand more times if it meant she'd make it home safe.

22

Ayden

The apartment's too quiet.

That's the first thing I notice when I drag myself out of bed. The kind of quiet that hums with tension instead of peace.

Serenity's already in the kitchen with a long-sleeved t-shirt and shorts, standing at the counter. She sets her coffee mug down and crosses her arm as soon as she hears my footsteps. Her silence feels heavier than any words she could throw.

I clear my throat. "Morning."

She doesn't look up. "Don't."

I exhale, leaning against the counter. "You're really not gonna talk to me?"

She turns then, eyes sharp. "You threw me over your shoulder in front of everyone, Ayden. You embarrassed me. What do you want me to say?"

"I wasn't gonna let you walk home alone."

"And I wasn't asking you to," she snaps. "You don't get to control me because you don't know how to deal with your own feelings."

I start to argue, but my phone buzzes on the counter.

I glance down.

And freeze.

Dad.

The name alone makes my jaw lock. He hasn't called in weeks. Not after our last fight. Not after the dinner with Serenity's parents. Not after anything.

My thumb hovers over *decline*—then I hit *accept* instead.

"Yeah," I say flatly.

A pause. Then that voice. Cold. Clipped. Distant. "I see you're still living with the Evans girl."

My grip on the phone tightens. "What do you want?"

Another pause. Paper shuffling. A sigh heavy with judgment. "I heard about the dinner."

"Of course you did."

"You embarrassed yourself. And me."

My jaw ticks. "If that's all, I've got somewhere to be."

"Don't hang up on me, Ayden."

But I already do.

The silence after the click is deafening. I stare at the phone like it's something venomous.

Serenity's watching me, brows knit together. "Who was it?"

I shove the phone in my pocket. "No one."

Her voice softens. "Ayden, you look—"

"I'm fine," I cut her off, sharper than I mean to.

She flinches. "Right. Sure."

I grab my jacket off the chair and head for the door.

"Where are you going?"

"Downtown," I mutter. "He wants to talk."

She hesitates. "Your dad?"

I nod once, still not looking at her.

"What did he say?"

"Nothing that matters."

I push out the door before she can stop me. The hallway air is colder, quieter. My chest still burns.

Because that's the thing about my dad—he never has to yell to make me angry.

All he has to do is *call*.

23

Ayden

The drive to Chicago feels longer than it should.

Thirty minutes isn't a lot of time — unless every minute feels like a countdown.

The road stretches out in front of me, gray and endless, the kind of overcast that makes the whole world look washed out. I roll the window down halfway, letting the cold air sting my face, hoping it'll clear my head. It doesn't.

The farther I get from Green Haven, the heavier it feels sitting in my chest.

Campus fades behind me — brick buildings, empty practice fields, the faint echo of laughter from the dorms — all replaced by the blur of traffic and billboards. The closer I get to the city, the more the air changes: thicker, grittier, alive with noise.

Chicago rises up in the distance like it's waiting for me.

Steel and glass cutting through the clouds, the skyline sharp enough to slice.

Every time I drive here, I tell myself I won't let him get to me again. And every damn time, I fail.

By the time I merge onto the Dan Ryan, I can feel my pulse ticking behind my eyes.

The radio's on, but I'm not listening. Just static and half-songs, a low hum that matches the noise in my head. My hand tightens on the steering wheel as I pass the same signs I've seen my whole life — exit markers, high rises, the stadium that used to mean everything to me.

I used to love this city.
Now it feels like every street corner remembers something I've tried to forget.

I take the exit toward downtown, weaving through the morning traffic, the buildings closing in around me. His office is on the 43rd floor of one of those perfect mirrored towers — the kind that look beautiful until you realize they reflect nothing but themselves.

I pull into a spot out front instead of the garage he pays for. He hates when I do that. Calls it "unprofessional."
Good.

Inside, everything smells like money — clean, cold, and empty. The receptionist gives me that polite, nervous look people always wear when they know my father's in one of his moods.

"Mr. Zander's expecting you," she says softly.

"Yeah," I mutter. "Lucky me."

The elevator ride up feels like standing in a pressure chamber. By the time the doors open, my stomach's tight, my jaw locked, and I'm already bracing for the storm.

He's waiting for me, back turned, staring out at the skyline like he owns it.

Same stance. Same tailored suit. Same perfect calm that always means danger.

"Close the door," he says without looking at me.

I do. Slowly.

"You wanted to see me," I say.

"George Evans called me this morning," he says. "Apparently you thought it was appropriate to raise your voice at him. At his own table."

I let out a humorless laugh. "Yeah, well, maybe if he wasn't busy insulting Serenity in front of everyone, I wouldn't have."

"You need to learn when to keep your mouth shut."

"No," I shoot back. "You mean I need to learn when to keep *your image* intact."

His jaw tightens. "That man has been good to me, Ayden. You wouldn't have half the opportunities you do without George's influence. You'd think you'd have learned to show a little gratitude."

"Gratitude?" I repeat, incredulous. "For what — for making deals with a guy who treats his daughter like property?"

His gaze sharpens. "Watch it."

I shake my head, anger rising fast. "You've been kissing that man's ass since before I could walk. You used him, just like you used everyone else. You made me play nice with his family, remember? You made me *date* Alix."

His expression doesn't even flicker. "Don't rewrite history, Ayden. You and Alix had a fine relationship."

"Fine?" I laugh, bitter. "It wasn't real. You made it happen. You told me if I didn't do it, I could kiss every scholarship and sponsorship goodbye. You told me it would 'keep things stable' between the families."

He exhales slowly, stepping around his desk. "You were a teenager. You don't understand how business works."

"I understood enough," I say, voice low. "I knew you didn't care who got hurt as long as you got your way."

His eyes narrow. "You benefited from that relationship."

"I *hated* that relationship," I snap. "Every day of it. I hated pretending. And I hated you for making me do it."

He takes a step forward, voice turning sharp. "I did what I had to do for your future. Everything I've ever done was to give you something better than what I had."

"Bullshit." My voice cracks on the word. "You did it for control. Because you can't stand the idea of me having something that isn't yours. Not my team. Not my life. Not Serenity."

His expression darkens, the calm in his voice vanishing. "That girl is going to ruin you."

"Maybe she'll save me from turning into you."

The silence that follows is electric. His hand twitches — I see it coming before it happens.

The crack of his palm against my cheek echoes through the room.

I don't flinch this time. I just stand there, cheek stinging, eyes burning into his.

"You don't talk to me like that," he says, low and deliberate.

"You don't *hit me* anymore," I growl.

For a second, we just stare at each other — years of unspoken things clawing their way up between us.

He's the first to look away. Adjusts his cufflinks. Straightens his tie. "You've lost perspective."

"No," I say. "I finally found it."

He sighs, already dismissing me. "You always were too emotional. It's why you'll never make it to the top."

I take a step toward the door, my jaw throbbing where he hit me. "If being like you is what it takes, I'll gladly stay at the bottom."

He doesn't say anything else. Doesn't even look up when I leave.

I walk out of that office with my cheek burning, my pulse pounding, and the faint taste of blood on my tongue.

Chicago hums outside, the horns, sirens, the heartbeat of a city that never cares who it crushes.
But at least out here, the air feels real.

For the first time in a long time, I don't look back.

24

Serenity

I didn't believe him when he said it was for therapy.

I should have known better.

Ayden had been acting suspicious all morning — nervous energy, quick glances, the kind of half-smile that meant he was hiding something.

We were supposed to complete our next "exposure exercise" for therapy: do something outside our comfort zones. When he pulled the envelope from his back pocket, I knew it.

"Lollapalooza?" I ask, staring at the wristbands like they might vanish.

He grins. "Consider it... therapeutic."

"Therapeutic?" I echo, raising an eyebrow. "You're telling me a festival with eighty thousand sweaty people is your idea of therapy?"

He shrugs, unbothered. "Crowds, music, emotional growth — it checks all the boxes."

"And you're sure it's not just because—"

He cuts me off, trying not to smile. "Because what?"

I give him a look. "Because it's almost my birthday?"

His grin slipped into something softer. "Maybe."

My eyebrows gather in confusion. "Wait a minute, Lolla is usually in August. It's practically the beginning of July?" I fold my arms across my chest, and raise one of my eyebrows throwing him a skeptical look.

He chuckles at my expression. "Stop deflecting, Iris. But I guess they needed to do it early or something this year. I have no clue, but we're going so go get dressed." He spins me around towards my room and gives me a push. Before my legs move to go change, Ayden gives my butt a light smack.

I give him my best glare, but all it does is make him laugh harder.

**

The train into Chicago was loud, humid, and alive.

Every seat is full with people in ripped jean shorts and colorful festival-esque get ups, carrying tote bags and disposable cameras. The city skyline rises ahead, shimmering in the heat, and I can feel my chest tighten—that familiar panic that always came with too much noise, too much movement.

Ayden notices. He reaches over and brushes his thumb against my hand — just enough to anchor me.

"You okay?"

I nod, though my throat feels tight. "Just breathing."

He doesn't let go.

When we step off the train at Grant Park, the sound hits me first—the layers of bass, shouting, laughter, the low hum of music spilling from every stage. The air was thick with sunscreen, sweat, and the smell of street food.

Ayden hands me a bottle of water like he'd planned this exact moment. "Drink," he says. "That's step one of surviving Lolla."

"Step two?"

"Let me handle the crowd."

He wasn't kidding. Every time the flow of people gets too close, he shifts slightly—not blocking me, exactly, but making sure I always had space. When someone bumps my shoulder, his hand finds the small of my back. When I freeze at the edge of a stage gate, he leans down and whispers, "Just focus on me."

So I did.

"In for four," he whispers. "Out for four. You're okay."

I match his rhythm, the sound of his voice cutting through the chaos until it's the only thing left. When my breathing steadies, he smiles — small, proud. "That's my girl."

Something in me melted, and it was quiet and dangerous.

By late afternoon, the sky had turned the color of burnt honey, and the city skyline glittered beyond the lake.

We found a spot near the front of one of the main stages, the crowd already thick.

Ayden checks his phone, trying and failing, to hide a grin.

"What?" I question curiously.

"You'll see," he said.

A hum rolls through the speakers — low, electric — and then I hear it: the first few notes of "End of Beginning."

"No way," I whisper.

Ayden grinned, his eyes catching the light. "Way."

The crowd roared as DJO walked on stage. I look up at him, my pulse racing. "You remembered."

He shrugs, but his voice is soft. "I remember everything about you."

The words hit deeper than I was ready for.

The crowd presses forward as the music swells. Ayden glances down at me, then crouches slightly, his back toward me.

"What are you doing?"

He looks over his shoulder, grinning. "You won't see anything from down here."

"Wait—"

"Come on." He reaches for my hand. "Dr. Adler says to face your fears, right?"

Before I can protest, his fingers slid around mine, warm and firm. "Trust me," he says, and something in his voice makes me forget to argue.

With a laugh that comes out half nervous, half exhilarated, I climb onto his back. He steadies me easily, his hands gripping my thighs, lifting me until I'm sitting on his shoulders.

The crowd around us blurs into motion — a sea of faces and hands and noise — and then suddenly, I can see everything.

The lights from the stage wash over the crowd in waves of violet and gold.

The lake glitters in the distance, reflecting the sunset.

The first line of the song ripples through the speakers:

"Just one more tear to cry, one teardrop from my eye..."

Ayden's hands tighten slightly against my legs as the bass kicked in, grounding me.

He looks up for a second, just long enough for our eyes to meet.

"Still okay?" he calls over the music.

"Yeah!" I laughed breathlessly. "Better than okay."

"Good." His smile breaks into something unguarded, wide and bright. "Then don't forget this."

The chorus hits, and the crowd screams the lyrics back to the stage.

I sing too, off-key and too loud, but it didn't matter. The sound of thousands of voices together felt like flying. Ayden keeps one hand steady on my calf, the other lifting occasionally to pump his fist in time with the beat. When I shift to get a better look, his hold tightens instinctively, his fingers pressing into my skin just enough to remind me I wasn't going anywhere.

I glance down, and the look on his face nearly knocks the air out of me.

He wasn't watching the stage.

He was watching me — his beautiful green eyes soft, his mouth tilted into a half-smile like he'd never seen anything quite like this.

The bridge hits, and he whispered up at me, his voice barely audible under the music. "Happy early birthday, Iris."

It felt like the whole world stopped.

My chest aches in the best way. "Thank you," I say, though I wasn't sure if he could hear me. He did. I saw it in the way his smile deepened — quiet, almost reverent.

When the final chorus hit—"Another version of me, I was in it..."— I realized that's what this was.

Another version of us.

After the set, when the crowd started to disperse, he helps me down slowly, his hands sliding down my sides to my waist as he steadies me. For a heartbeat, we don't move.

His forehead brushes against mine.

Neither of us speak.

The world is still humming around us — laughter, distant fireworks, someone singing along to a different stage — but in that moment, it feels like everything else is muted.

"You okay?" he murmurs.

I nod. "Yeah. I think so."

"Good." His thumb brushes just above my hip before he lets go.

We stay there a little longer, watching the lights fade into the dark. Then he drapes his hoodie over my shoulders. It smells like rain and cedar and the faint sweetness of whatever cologne he'd borrowed from Ryan. As we walk back toward the exit, our fingers brush once, twice, before finally finding each other and staying that way. Neither of us say it, but we both know; this night matters.

And maybe, for the first time, it feels real between us.

25

Serenity

The sound of Beck's laughter fills the living room, loud and contagious, bouncing off the walls. Luke's sprawled across the armchair, sipping a soda, while Ryan's sitting upside down on the couch — legs hanging over the backrest, head nearly touching the floor.

"So," Beck says, grinning, "we're thinking fireworks at the lake again, right? Like last year?"

Ryan tilts his head back, his laughter filling the space. "Last year, Beck nearly blew off her hand lighting one."

Beck throws a pillow at him. "That was an accident!"

Luke laughs. "That was stupidity, not an accident."

I smile faintly, watching them argue. It's easy; the teasing, the noise, the feeling that we're still just a bunch of college kids figuring out life one laugh at a time.

But then Luke looks over at me. "You coming this year, Ren?"

"Yeah," Beck adds, still grinning. "You totally skipped out last time. You don't get to ditch us again."

I force a small smile. "Yeah. Maybe."

"Maybe?" Ryan sits up. "What, you got better plans?"

I shake my head quickly. "No, I just..."

My voice trails off. The sound of fireworks in the distance; sounds like someone testing them early, pops through the open window. It shouldn't mean anything, but it hits something deep.

One year.

One year since everything changed.

I blink hard, but the room's already fading — Beck's laughter, Luke's teasing, all replaced by the echo of another summer night.

one year AGO

The gym smelled like sweat and old polish that night.
The sound of a basketball bouncing off the hardwood drew me closer down the hallway. I was smiling, rehearsing something stupid in my head — something about wanting to see him for the Fourth.

I never got the words out.

Alix's voice reached me first, light and sharp. "You know she's obsessed with you, right? Serenity. She's practically in love with you."

I froze just outside the door.

Ayden sighed. "Alix, drop it."

"She's pathetic," Alix went on, ignoring him. "Following you around, hanging on your every word. It's embarrassing."

The air left my lungs.

Then Ayden said it. His voice low, tired — and cold.
"She doesn't mean anything to me, Alix. She's just your annoying little sister."

I didn't feel my heart break. Not at first. It was quieter than that.
Just a slow, sinking kind of hurt that started in my chest and spread everywhere else.

Alix laughed, that bright, polished sound that never reached her eyes. "Good. I was starting to think you actually cared."

I couldn't listen anymore.

I turned and walked out the same way I came in, trying not to make a sound. The gym doors shut softly behind me, but it felt loud — final.

Outside, the air was thick with smoke and fireworks, laughter drifting from the quad. Someone shouted my name from a distance, but I kept walking until I hit the lake.

That night, I watched the fireworks alone, colors exploding across the water, and told myself it didn't matter.
That I didn't care.
That maybe Ayden had never meant to.

Three days later, I turned twenty.
And he didn't even text me.

"Earth to Serenity," Beck's voice cuts through the fog of memory.

I blink and look up. They're all staring at me. Luke's brow furrows, concerned. "You okay, Ren? You zoned out for a sec."

"Yeah," I say quickly, forcing a small smile. "Just...thinking."

Ryan tosses another pillow at Beck. "Probably about how boring you are."

Beck catches it, grinning, and just like that the room comes back to life — laughter, noise, easy comfort.

But inside, that old ache hums quietly; the memory of fireworks, of words I can't forget, and a boy who looked at me like I was everything once...then called me nothing.

26
Ayden

ONE YEAR AGO

The Fourth of July was supposed to be simple.

Team hangout at the gym, fireworks at the lake, a few hours of pretending I wasn't living two different lives.

But nothing was simple when Alix was involved.

She'd shown up right as I was finishing practice — heels clicking against the court, perfume too strong, smile too sharp. The sight of her alone was enough to make my chest tighten.

Because every time I saw her, I saw him.

My father.

He was the reason we were together.

He was the reason I couldn't look Serenity in the eye any-more.

"Ayden," Alix said, her voice syrup-sweet as she leaned against the bleachers. "You've been avoiding me."

"I've been busy," I muttered, grabbing my water bottle.

"Busy ignoring me?" she teased, but there was an edge under the joke. "Or busy sneaking around with my sister?"

I froze.

She smiled, slow and venomous. "You really think I don't notice the way she looks at you? The way you look back?"

"I don't—" I started, but she cut me off.

"My dad likes you," she continued. "Your dad needs my dad. You mess this up, and both of them are going to have something to say about it."

That landed like a punch to the gut. She wasn't wrong. My father had been riding me for months — "Play nice with Alix," "Stay in control," "Don't get distracted by her sister."

But I already was.
Completely.

Serenity was the one person who made all of this mess feel bearable — the only thing in my life that felt real.
And that terrified him.
Which meant it terrified me, too.

"Alix," I said finally, rubbing the back of my neck. "Can we not do this right now?"

She crossed her arms, tilting her head. "You know she has feelings for you, right? Everyone can see it. It's pathetic."

I looked up sharply. "Don't talk about her like that."

Her smirk widened. "Then what should I say? That you like her back? That the great Ayden Miller can't stop thinking about his girlfriend's little sister?"

"Alix, stop."

"Or maybe," she went on, voice dropping, "I should tell your father where you've really been after practice. You think he'd like knowing you're risking everything he's built for some crush?"

Something snapped in me then — not anger, not pride. Fear.

That same sick, suffocating fear that always came when my dad's shadow got too close.

I didn't think. I just reacted.

"She doesn't mean anything to me, Alix," I said, the words leaving my mouth like poison. "She's just your annoying little sister."

The second they were out, I wanted to claw them back.

But Alix smiled — that cold, satisfied smile that made my skin crawl. "Good," she said. "Because I was starting to think you actually cared."

And then I heard it — the smallest sound behind me. A quiet, broken inhale.

I turned.

Serenity stood just inside the doorway, frozen, eyes wide, tears shining under the fluorescent lights.

"Serenity—"

But she was already backing away, shaking her head like she couldn't believe it.

Her voice was barely a whisper. "Don't."

Then she turned and ran.

"Serenity!" I called after her, but the door slammed before I could move.

The silence that followed was deafening.

When I finally looked back, Alix was smirking again. "Guess she got the message."

I wanted to yell, to say it wasn't true, to chase Serenity down and tell her everything — about my father, about the deal, about how every word I'd just said was a lie.

But all I could do was stand there, fists clenched, heart pounding, knowing I'd just become exactly what my father wanted me to be.

Cold. Controlled.

And completely alone.

Outside, the fireworks started.

And for the first time in my life, I hated the sound of them.

27
Serenity

The Fourth of July always brings too much noise. Fireworks. Music. Laughter that feels a little too forced. And memories that won't stay buried.

This year is no different.

Beck's the first one in the apartment—my favorite chaos in human form. She bursts through the door with two popsicles and a grin that's way too bright for the humidity.

"Lake trip, twenty minutes," she says, shoving a popsicle into my hand. "Luke and Ryan already texted. You're not backing out this time."

I smirk. "What makes you think I want to go?"

She raises an eyebrow. "Because you need to. And because if you stay here, Ayden won't go either."

Right on cue, his door opens. Ayden steps out, pulling a black hoodie over his head, hair messy, eyes tired. He looks effortlessly good in the way that always annoys me.

Beck grins at him. "Good. You're coming too."

He gives her a flat look. "I didn't say that."

"You didn't have to," she says, grabbing her keys. "See you there!"

And then she's gone — leaving the air between me and Ayden heavy, the way it always gets when we're alone too long.

He glances at me. "You really want to go?"

"Do you?"

He hesitates, then shrugs. "Guess we should. People are expecting us."

That one word; *us,* makes something flutter in my stomach I wish I could kill.

Because it's not real.

It's never been real.

Not the holding hands, not the lingering glances, not the way everyone thinks we're together.

The whole *fake dating* thing started weeks ago. We agreed it was harmless—good for his image.

But every time he smiles for show, every time he touches my waist like it's part of an act...it feels too close to the lie I once believed.

***

The lake is alive with sound when we get there.

Laughter, music, the soft crack of sparklers. The smell of smoke clings to everything.

Beck, Luke, and Ryan are already sprawled on a blanket near the dock, talking over each other. Beck tosses me a soda, smirking. "See? Not so bad."

I sit down beside her, pretending to agree. Ayden settles on my other side, close enough that I can feel the heat from his arm, but not close enough to touch.

When the fireworks start, the crowd's cheers blend with the hum of cicadas and the faint lap of water against the dock. Gold and red burst across the sky, lighting Ayden's face in color.

He looks up, quiet, unreadable. "You still hate this day?"

I glance at him. "Maybe."

He studies me for a second. "You didn't used to."

"I didn't used to have a reason to."

Something flickers in his eyes—guilt, maybe. "Serenity—"

"Don't," I cut him off.

But he doesn't stop. "I never explained what happened last year."

"There's nothing to explain."

He shakes his head, jaw tight. "There is. You heard me say something I didn't mean."

"I heard exactly what you meant," I whisper. "You said I didn't matter. That I was just Alix's annoying little sister."

His voice drops. "I had to. My dad was in my ear every second. He was using her, using me, trying to control everything—"

"You still let him," I snap. "You still said it."

He runs a hand through his hair. "You don't get it. There's still so much that you don't know, Serenity."

"Don't spin this into protection," I say quietly. "You never told me you liked me, Ayden. You never said anything."

He meets my eyes. "Because I wasn't supposed to."

"Then what is this?" I gesture between us. "This fake dating thing—what are we doing? I mean, every time I'm around you I feel like a have whiplash from your mood swings."

"It was supposed to be a lie," he admits, his voice low. "But it hasn't felt fake for me in a while."

The world seems to tilt. The fireworks paint his face in bursts of gold and violet, his gaze burning through the dark.

"Don't," I whisper, shaking my head. "Don't look at me like that. Not when it's not real."

He lets out a short, shaky laugh, more pain than humor. "You really think this is fake?"

He moves closer before I can answer, the air between us charged. "You drive me insane, Serenity. You always have."

"Stop—"

"No," he says, voice raw. "I'm done stopping."

And then a growl escapes his lips, "Fuck it."

Before I can breathe, his hand is in my hair, his other on my jaw, and his mouth is on mine.

It's not careful. It's not soft.
It's everything we've been pretending not to feel—anger, regret, longing—all crashing together like the fireworks exploding above us.

For a second, I kiss him back. I can't help it.
His lips are warm, desperate, and it feels like coming up for air after a year of drowning.

But then reality hits.

The same words he said a year ago echo in my head—*She doesn't mean anything to me.*

I break away, breathless, shaking. "Ayden, stop."

He's still close, his forehead resting against mine, voice quiet and wrecked. "Tell me you didn't feel that."

I step back, my chest aching. "I can't do this. You can't just kiss me because you feel guilty."

He looks at me like I've just gutted him. "That's not why I did it."

"Then why?"

He opens his mouth, but nothing comes out. Just silence. And that silence is worse than any lie.

Behind us, the crowd cheers as the finale begins—fireworks bursting brighter, louder, like the whole sky's on fire.

I turn away, whispering, "You'll only break me again."

He doesn't try to stop me.

When I walk off the dock, the noise of the fireworks fades behind me, replaced by the sound of my heartbeat pounding in my ears.

Because even now, after everything— a part of me wanted him to mean it.

28

Ayden

The fireworks are still going off when Serenity walks away.

I stay there on the dock, watching her disappear into the crowd — the back of her hair glowing in the gold light of the finale.

I don't move.

I can't.

The cheers fade, the bursts slow, and the night quiets again, leaving only the smell of smoke and the hollow echo of what I just did.

I kissed her.

After a year of holding everything back, after a year of telling myself she deserved better, I finally broke.

And she walked away — again.

I can still taste her lip gloss, still feel the tremble in her breath before she pulled back.

And the worst part?

I'd do it again in a heartbeat.

By the time I make it back to the apartment, the air's cooled and the adrenaline's worn off, leaving nothing but that familiar ache in my chest.

Beck's waiting for me in the kitchen, sitting cross-legged on the counter like she owns the place — hair messy, fireworks glow still faintly on her cheeks.

She looks up when the door shuts. "You look like you got hit by a truck."

"Close," I mutter, running a hand through my hair.

"Where's Serenity?"

"She left. She's probably staying at the bookstore tonight. "

Beck frowns. "You two fought?"

"Not exactly."

"Then what happened?"

I hesitate. She narrows her eyes, already reading me. "Oh my God. You kissed her, didn't you?"

I look away. "Beck—"

Her jaw drops. "You *did*! Holy shit, Ayden." She hops down from the counter, half laughing, half horrified. "Finally, and also... seriously? Now?"

I don't answer.

She studies me for a second, the teasing fading when she catches my expression. "She didn't kiss you back, did she?"

"She did," I say quietly. "For a second."

Then I shake my head. "But she pulled away. Said I'd break her again."

Beck's face softens. "Ayden..."

"I shouldn't have done it," I say, pacing. "I've screwed this up every way possible. Last year, I hurt her. This year, I kissed her like it would fix everything."

"It's not about fixing it," Beck says gently. "It's about being honest for once."

I stop pacing. "You think she wants honesty from me now? She doesn't even trust me."

"Then earn it," she says simply.

I laugh under my breath, bitter. "You make it sound easy."

"It's not," she says, stepping closer. "But you can't keep dancing around it. She's not stupid, Ayden. She knows you care about her."

I meet her eyes. "That's the problem. She *thinks* I care. She doesn't know."

Beck crosses her arms. "Then tell her."

I scoff. "Yeah, because saying 'Hey, sorry I broke your heart, lied about it, and kissed you like an idiot' will totally go over well."

"Not like that, genius," she says, rolling her eyes. "You need to stop trying to explain and just *show* her."

I frown. "Show her how?"

She smirks — that mischievous Beck kind of smirk that means she's already plotting something dangerous and heartfelt at the same time.

"I've got an idea," she says.

I raise an eyebrow. "You planning to humiliate me?"

"Probably," she says lightly. "But it'll work."

"Beck—"

She holds up a hand. "Nope. Don't argue. You've been miserable for a year, and she's been pretending she's over you when she's clearly not. You two need a reset — something real. Let me handle it."

I shake my head but can't help the faint smile that creeps up. "You're insane."

"Runs in the family," she says with a grin. Then, softer, "You love her, don't you?"

The question hits harder than I expect.
It's not the first time someone's asked me, but it's the first time I don't dodge it.

I let out a breath. "Yeah. I do."

Beck's smile fades into something genuine. "Then you'll figure it out. We will."

I nod slowly, the first spark of something that almost feels like hope stirring in my chest.

"Alright," she says, hopping off the counter and grabbing her keys. "Get some sleep. You're gonna need it."

I frown. "Why?"

She just smirks again. "Because tomorrow, we start Operation Don't Let Ayden Die Alone."

"Beck—"

"Goodnight, lover boy."

The door clicks shut behind her before I can say another word.

I sink onto the couch, rubbing a hand over my face. The room's quiet again — just the hum of the fridge and the faint sound of fireworks still echoing in the distance.

I don't know what Beck's planning, but for the first time in a long time, I don't feel completely lost.

Because she's right.

It's time to stop hiding behind fear and mistakes.

It's time to show Serenity what I should've said a long time ago.

29

Serenity

Dress - Taylor Swift

Birthdays stopped feeling special a long time ago.

The morning starts quietly — sunlight spilling through the bookstore windows, dust motes floating like slow confetti. The bell above the door jingles a few times throughout the day. A couple of regulars stop in. Mrs. Collins picks up her weekly romance novels. Two college kids argue over which Stephen King book to buy.

It's calm, peaceful. Just how I like it.

But by the time the clock hits eight, I'm starting to feel it — that quiet ache that comes from too much silence.

My phone buzzes against the counter.

> Luke: Happy birthday, Ren! Come out tonight!

> Ryan: Hope Beck drags you tonight You deserve some fun!

> Beck: Bitch, you better get out of that dusty bookstore and have some fun on your 21st birthday! My offer to take you downtown still stands btw. Just let me know, ily bitch

No message from Ayden.

I tell myself it doesn't matter. That he's probably busy. That I shouldn't expect anything from him anymore.

But it still stings. Because no matter how much I try to move on, some part of me always waits for *him*.

I sigh, locking my phone and turning the sign on the door to *Closed*.

The store feels warmer at night — the way it always does when the lights dim and Green Haven quiets outside. I start shelving the last stack of returns, wandering toward the back of the classics section.

The smell of old paper and cedar fills the air. I run my fingers along the spines — Austen, Brontë, Fitzgerald — until I stop on a shelf halfway down.

The books there are older, worn, their covers soft from years of use.

And then I see it:

Our initials; our first names and middle names **S.E. + A.J** .—carved into the spine of Les Misérables, the ink faded but still there. We must've been fourteen. Maybe fifteen. Back when Ayden used to spend nights here when things got bad with Alix, or worse — at home. Before my Grams got sick, she always used to let Ayden and I assemble makeshift forts in the back of the store and sleepover. My heart tightens at the memories; of my Grams and Ayden.

The memory flashes bright: him curled up on the floor beside me, both of us reading under the same blanket fort, pretending the world outside didn't exist. Like for a few hours all that mattered was us.

A lump rises in my throat.

I move a few books over, fingers brushing against another —*The Great Gatsby*.

My all-time favorite.

This one's different — a special edition, deep green with gold lettering, one I've never seen before. There's a note tucked inside the front cover. My name is written across it in his handwriting.

My breath catches.

I unfold it slowly, hands shaking.

You're my green light at the end of the dock, Serenity. Love, Ayden.

My vision blurs instantly. Because he said those same words once before — two nights before everything fell apart, when I pretended to be asleep on the bookstore couch and he whispered it into the dark, thinking I was asleep.

"You're my green light at the end of the dock, Serenity."

I remember the sound of his voice back then — soft and trembling, like he wasn't supposed to say it out loud. And now, seeing it in writing, a year later, after everything...it breaks something open in me I thought had long since closed.

The tears come before I can stop them. I sink down to the floor, the note clutched to my chest, the smell of old books and candle wax filling the air.

When I finally find the strength to move, I wander toward the back room near the old lounge where I keep the couch and a few blankets.

Except tonight, it's different.

There are candles scattered across the floor, small flames flickering inside glass jars. A soft glow spills over the blankets spread out on the rug, fairy lights woven through the shelves behind it.

My heartbeat stumbles.

"What..." I whisper to no one.

The bell above the door chimes softly.

I turn.

Ayden.

He's dressed better than I've ever seen him — dark jeans, a fitted long-sleeved white dress shirt, his dark hair slightly pushed back but still falling slightly into his eyes. His green eyes are shining with determination, like he came here for one thing and one thing only—me.

"Hey," he whispers.

My voice barely works. "What is this?"

He closes the door behind him, hands in his pockets. "You didn't really think I forgot your birthday, did you?"

I blink, still holding the note. "Ayden, I—"

He walks closer, slow and careful, like he's afraid one wrong move will make me run. "I found that copy of *The Great Gatsby* months ago. The same edition you wouldn't shut up about years ago."

My breathe catches in my throat as I glance down at the note. "You remembered."

"I remember everything," he says softly.

The air between us hums with that familiar electricity — the same tension that's always been there, just quieter now, older, heavier.

"I needed to tell you something," he continues, stopping just a few feet away. "Something I should've said a long time ago."

"Ayden..."

He shakes his head. "Just let me finish, okay?"

His voice wavers, but his eyes don't leave mine. "Alix and I's relationship was never real. It was fake from the very beginning. I went along with it because I was stupid and scared. But I swear to you, Serenity, none of it meant anything."

I feel my chest tighten, my heart hammering against my ribs. Oh my god. It was never real. My mind races with every question, and I can't bring myself to ask any of them. Not right now.

He steps closer, barely a foot between us now. "You were the only thing that did."

The candles flicker, and for a moment, it feels like the whole world has gone quiet.

He's standing there, hands in his pockets, that same careful expression that used to drive me crazy — like he's trying not to set me off but already knows it's too late.

"Why are you here, Ayden?" My voice shakes. "What is this?"

"I told you," he says quietly. "I needed to see you."

I laugh, bitter and sharp. "That's funny. You didn't need to see me when you told Alix I didn't mean anything to you."

His jaw tightens. "You're still holding onto that?"

"How could I not?" I snap. "You said it like it was easy."

He takes a step closer. "You don't understand what was happening—"

"Oh, don't give me that," I cut in. "I *heard* you. I don't need an explanation to know what it feels like to be humiliated by the only person I—"

"Don't," he interrupts, his voice breaking a little.

My throat tightens. "Don't what? Tell the truth?"

"No," he says, taking another step forward, eyes locked on mine. "Don't act like that night didn't destroy me too."

I shake my head, blinking away the sting behind my eyes. "You got to move on. You got to hide behind your perfect reputation while I got to look like the girl who couldn't take a hint."

"Serenity—"

"Don't," I whisper. "You don't get to say my name like that anymore."

Something in him snaps.

In two strides, he's in front of me, his hand finding mine, his other braced against the shelf behind me. The sudden movement makes my back press softly against the rows of books. My breath catches.

He's close — so close I can feel the warmth radiating off him. His voice is low, trembling but sure.

"I've spent a year trying not to touch you, not to look at you, not to *want* you — and it's killing me. "

My pulse stumbles. "You don't get to say that now."

"I'm saying it because it's true," he says, his forehead nearly brushing mine. "I messed up. I lied. I hurt you. But I never stopped—"

He cuts himself off, exhaling hard.

"Never stopped what?" I whisper.

His eyes flick to my mouth. "Feeling everything I wasn't supposed to."

The air between us crackles. My hand trembles against his chest, the beat of his heart fast under my palm.

"This doesn't fix anything," I whisper, my voice unsteady.

"I know," he murmurs. "But maybe it's a start."

Then he closes the distance.

The kiss hits like gravity finally giving in — fierce, desperate, years of emotion crashing into one breath. His hand slides up my jaw, fingers curling at the nape of my neck, his body pressing just enough against me to make me feel the weight of everything we've been holding back. My lips part as a moan escapes me, and he takes the opportunity to slip his tongue into my mouth, deepening the kiss.

His hands leave a burning trail; roaming my body, tracing the curves of my waist and the swell of my hips. I feel the cold wood of the bookshelf against my back not for long as Ayden pulls me forward, one arm wrapped around my waist, the other desperately trying to find the hem of my dress. His hand finally finds it and without a second thought he lifts it off of me and above my head, only to throw it somewhere in the distance.

And there I was before him in my black lace bra and panties set, and the look in his eyes as he takes in the sight of me makes me feel like the most beautiful girl in the universe.

He leans in again, his lips finding the most sensitive spot on my neck right below my ear, his hands cupping my breasts. I moan, my head falling back against the bookshelf; the creak of the books against my weight. He unhooks my bra, discarding it just like my dress. His hands cup my breasts again, his thumbs brushing against my nipples and I arch into his touch, my body on fire.

His hands move to my panties and he hooks his fingers into the waistband, pulling them down. He sets me down lightly on my feet so I can step out of them, his eyes never leaving mine. I can't tell if it's the cold air in the bookstore or the way he's looking at me that sends a shiver up my spine; but I don't care: I would give up the whole world to have him look at me like this everyday for the rest of our lives.

We lock eyes as he sinks to his knees, his hands spreading my thighs. "I'm not doing anything until I taste this pretty pussy, baby." He lifts me again, only this time, he stays kneeling and my legs are on either side of his head leaving me bare and spread open for him. He holds my gaze as his lips form the most devilish smirk. "You'd better hold on tight, Iris. I'm not stopping until you come on my face and the only word coming from those pretty lips is my name on repeat like a prayer."

I gasp at his words and his tongue as it's found my clit. He licks and sucks, his tongue swirling around my most sensitive spot, the act alone is my source of undoing. I moan loudly, my hands gripping the bookshelf for support, one of the books falling to the floor with a bang. I feel the pleasure building like waves crashing against the ocean, my body tensing as I near the edge.

"Oh my god, Ayden!" I scream as my hand shoot forward to grip his hair. He looks up at me, those green eyes filled with pure desire that burns through me on the spot.

"Go ahead let it go, baby," he whispers, his deep voice filled with need.

And I do. I come undone and let it go, my body convulsing as the waves of pleasure wash over me. He continues to lick and suck, drawing out my orgasm until I'm a trembling mess and the feeling in my legs are gone.

He stands up, pulling me back into his arms my legs wrapped around his waist. His lips find mine in a deep, passionate kiss. I groan as I taste myself on his lips. He breaks the kiss briefly as his hands move to his jeans to unbutton them and push them down his legs along with his underwear. I see his erection; hard and ready. He positions himself at my entrance, his eyes never leaving mine.

"Are you sure about this? There's no going back if we do this," Ayden pants, searching my eyes for any signs of doubt. I grip either side of his face, smiling.

"I'm sure, Ayden."

His eyes drop from my face down to where we're almost connected before his lips meet mine for a soul-taking kiss.

"Serenity," he murmurs, his voice full of love and desire. "I love you."

My heart fills with so much love I'm surprised it isn't bursting out of my chest.

"I love you too," I whisper.

He pushes into me, filling me completely. I gasp, my body stretching to accommodate him. He begins to move, his hips thrusting against mine. He moves slowly at first, like he doesn't want to break me. I feel every inch of him, every thrust sending waves of pleasure through my body. His head drops to the crook of my neck as he lets out a deep moan, my name escaping his lips over and over. His thrusts become more urgent. I feel the same pressure building, the need to release overtakes my body. Ayden peppers kisses up my jaw and over my cheeks, breathing heavily.

"Come with me, Iris," he breathes.

And for the second time tonight, I come, the pleasure washing over me. Ayden continues thrusting; his body moving faster, his breath coming in short gasps. I feel every muscle of his tensing, his body over the edge.

He comes with a guttural groan so deep, his head falling back, his body shuddering as he fills me. I hold him close as we both ride out the orgasm, panting hard.

He's still kissing along my neck and jaw as we move from the bookshelf and up the stairs to my old room above the bookstore. The touch of his hands holding my thighs as we reach the top of the stairs will forever be burned into my memory. Ayden finally reaches my old room in the upstairs apartment, and I go flying onto the bed.

"Did you really just throw me, asshole?" I throw a pillow at his head, but he dodges it and tackles me, his fingers tickling my sides.

We finally settle once he tires out from my constant squirming. He scoots back and grabs me, wrapping his strong arms around my waist as I lay my head on his chest. My eyes roam over his assortment of tattoos once we lock opposite hands, our fingers interlocked. My eyes lock on the small blue butterfly on the inside of his bicep that has small cursive lettering with the name Iris. My eyebrows furrow in confusion. *What is his obsession with the name 'Iris'?*

Before I can stop it, my free hand reaches out, lightly tracing the tattoo. Ayden muscles tighten at first at my touch, but then relax.

"Why do you love the name Iris so much? Do you have a secret ex-girlfriend that I don't know about or something?" I half-joke, my curiosity peeking.

Ayden swipes a curl away from my shoulder and starts rubbing circles mindlessly across my skin.

"It's not so much a name to me, it's a special meaning for something; someone." He hooks a finger under my chin, slowly bringing my eyes up to meet his. His expression is dead serious—no hint of playfulness behind it whatsoever. His finger trails from my chin up to my cheek, leaving behind a trail of goosebumps at his tender touch.

"Have you ever heard of the song 'Iris' by The Goo Goo Dolls?"

I roll my eyes. "I don't live under a rock Ayden James Zander. Of course," That earns me a playful tug on my hair. I let out a giggle, but quickly stop because he seems so serious right now.

"Continue."

He sarcastically rolls his eyes at me before speaking again. "Like I was saying, it was the night we fell asleep downstairs in the bookstore two years ago—my dad and I had fought that night and the only place I could think to come to was here; to be with you. The whole way here I played Iris on repeat and when I got here—to you, you're the only person that mattered. Even though I was made to be broken, you still saw me. The real me; and you've loved me unconditionally from the moment we met as kids." He looks down at the tattoo his eyes glistening with fresh tears, but before they can fall, he stops them and sniffles.

"That's why I call you Iris, and that's why I have this tattoo; to remind me no matter how broken I feel, I'll always have your love to put me back together."

I can't say anything. I'm entirely and utterly speechless. I open my mouth to something, anything—but nothing comes out but a sob. I cry into his neck as he holds me and just lets me get everything I'm feeling out. His hand lightly combs through my curls, which helps me calm down. I guess he calms me down too much, because shortly I start to fall asleep. I feel him place a soft kiss against my forehead before my eyes close for the most peaceful sleep I've had in years.

30
Serenity

The first thing I feel is warmth.

Not the kind from the morning sun, but the kind that comes from skin, breath, and quiet.

Ayden's arm is draped around me, heavy and loose, his hand resting against my waist. I can feel his heartbeat through the stillness — slow, steady, real.

For a long time, I just lie there and breathe.

The smell of him clings to the blanket — cedar, soap, a little smoke from the candles that burned down to glass jars on the floor. The bookstore looks different in daylight.

Softer. Golden. The shelves glow in the sun pouring through the big front windows, and the air smells like coffee and old pages. My old bed creaks when I shift.

Last night rushes back like a wave.

The argument.

The way everything finally cracked open — all the hurt, all the years of pretending we didn't still want each other.

The moment we stopped fighting it.

It wasn't rushed or reckless; it was quiet and aching and real.

The way he held me after, like it was the only thing he was sure of.

The way he whispered my name like it was an apology and a prayer in one breath.

I blink back the tears that sting behind my eyes.

Because for the first time, it didn't feel like we were breaking something.

It felt like we were finally putting it back together.

Ayden stirs behind me, his voice rough with sleep. "You're thinking too loud."

I smile faintly. "I'm allowed."

He shifts so he can see me, his face half-shadowed by the morning light. His hair's a mess, his voice softer than I've ever heard it. "You okay?"

"I think so," I whisper.

He studies me for a moment — not the way people look when they're trying to figure you out, but the way someone does when they already know.

"You're staring," I say.

He smiles. "You look... peaceful."

"Shocked, honestly."

He laughs quietly. "Why?"

I shrug, tracing the edge of the blanket. "Because for a long time, I thought if we ever ended up here, it'd be a mistake."

"And now?" he asks.

I meet his eyes. "Now it just feels right."

Something in his expression softens. He brushes a strand of hair from my face, his fingertips trailing gently against my skin. "You're still mad at me, aren't you?"

"Mad might be a strong word," I say. "Deeply suspicious, maybe."

He grins — that lopsided one that always used to get to me. "I'll take it."

We fall into an easy silence. The kind that used to feel impossible between us. His thumb moves slowly along the back of my hand, tracing circles that make it hard to think straight.

Then, because I can't help myself, I tease, "So... was this your plan all along? Show up, start a fight, make a grand speech, and..."

He groans, burying his face in the crook of my neck. "You make it sound manipulative."

I laugh softly. "Wasn't it?"

"Not exactly," he says, voice muffled. "I just wanted you to know the truth. Everything else kind of... happened."

I grin. "Kind of?"

He looks up, eyes glinting. "Fine, Serenity Elora Evans. It was always in my evil master plan to fuck you against a bookshelf. It's always been a dream of mine," he drawls on sarcastically, trying to keep his laughter in but fails, bursting out laughing.

My cheeks heat, but I can't stop smiling. "You're impossible."

"Yeah," he says, leaning closer, his voice low and teasing, "but you like me that way."

I roll my eyes, but my heart feels light. It's strange — we've spent so long walking on eggshells, afraid of the past, afraid of each other. But now, sitting here wrapped in morning light and leftover candle smoke, it feels... easy.

Like this was always supposed to happen.

Ayden stretches, then stands, tugging his hoodie on halfway before giving up and ruffling his hair instead. "We should probably get actual food before Beck stages a rescue mission."

"She's going to kill you when she finds out where you were last night."

He laughs. "She'll survive. She's been plotting this for months anyway."

I throw a pillow at him. "You're not funny."

He catches it midair, grinning. "You're smiling."

"Shut up."

"Make me."

I shake my head, laughing again. "You're seriously proud of yourself, huh?"

He steps closer, that mischievous glint softening into something warmer. "Not proud," he says quietly. "Just... grateful."

I meet his gaze, the teasing fading. "For what?"

"For this. For you."

And just like that, the world quiets again.

He leans down, presses his forehead against mine, and whispers, "Happy birthday, Serenity."

I close my eyes, letting out a shaky breath. "You already said that last night."

"Then I'll keep saying it," he teases.

The sun shifts higher through the window, spilling light across our faces, and for the first time in what feels like forever, I let myself believe in us — not the memory, not the pain — just this moment.

Simple, warm, and real.

***

For the first time in a long time, the bookstore feels alive again.

Sunlight spills through the windows, lighting up the dust motes in the air. The smell of coffee and old books mixes with something new — laughter.

Mine and Ayden's.

He's behind the counter making coffee, pretending he knows what he's doing. The espresso machine makes an aggressive hiss, and he jumps back like it's possessed.

I laugh so hard I nearly spill the mug I'm holding. "You're hopeless."

He glares at the machine like it personally offended him. "Why is it steaming like that? Is this thing broken?"

"It's called pressure, genius."

"Yeah, well, it's pressuring *me*."

I giggle. "Maybe it just doesn't like people who can't tell a latte from a light roast. Figure out what you want first!"

He grins, leaning against the counter. "Oh, I know what I want."

The look he gives me makes my heart skip, and I roll my eyes quickly before he can see how much it still affects me. "You're such a flirt."

"Admit it. You missed me."

"Not even a little."

"You're lying."

"Maybe."

We're still smirking at each other when the bell above the door rings.

"Helloooo?" Beck's voice sings through the air, followed by the sound of her boots squeaking on the floor. "Anyone alive in this house of nerds?"

Ayden groans under his breath. "Here we go."

Beck appears at the end of the aisle a second later, wearing her usual chaos — a bright red hoodie and sunglasses even though it's cloudy outside. She stops dead in her tracks when she sees us behind the counter together.

Her grin widens like a cat spotting something shiny. "Well, well, well. Look who's actually smiling for once."

"Morning, Beck," I say, trying to sound casual.

"Morning, my favorite lovebirds," she says sweetly, drawing out the word until I want to disappear behind the counter.

Ayden groans. "Beck—"

"Don't you *Beck* me," she says, waving a finger at him. "Do you have *any idea* how long I've been waiting for this? The slow burn.

The angst. The enemies-to-lovers energy. It's been a full-time job keeping my mouth shut."

I snort, covering my mouth to hide a laugh. "You? Keep your mouth shut? Impossible."

She gasps dramatically. "Wow. The betrayal. I help you two emotionally stunted people find love, and this is how I'm repaid?"

Ayden crosses his arms. "You didn't do anything."

"Excuse me?" Beck points at the ceiling. "Who forced you to go to the lake? Who told Serenity to *actually* talk to you instead of glaring from across the living room? You're welcome."

I shake my head, smiling despite myself. "You're unbelievable."

Beck flops onto one of the armchairs with the grace of a falling cat. "So? Did you two finally admit your undying love? Or do I need to cue dramatic background music again?"

Ayden groans. "You're not funny."

"Oh, I'm hilarious," Beck says, pointing at me. "You're just cranky because I walked in on your little morning date."

"It wasn't a date," I say quickly, too quickly.

Beck raises a brow, smug. "Oh really? Because you're both glowing like you just got hit with a Hallmark filter."

Ayden mutters, "I regret every decision that led to this moment."

She laughs, leaning forward. "No, you don't. You finally stopped being miserable. I call that progress."

He sighs, but there's a small smile tugging at his mouth. "You're impossible."

Beck stands, clapping her hands. "Alright, enough romantic tension. Birthday girl, go get dressed. We're closing early tonight."

I blink. "Why?"

She smirks. "Because I'm throwing you a party, obviously. Luke and Ryan are already in. Don't argue."

Ayden and I exchange a look — the kind that says *we're in trouble but it's too late to fight it.*

"Beck—" I start.

"Don't 'Beck' me either," she says, wagging her finger at both of us. "Be ready by seven. Both of you."

And before either of us can respond, she's already halfway out the door, calling over her shoulder, "Wear something cute! I expect fireworks — metaphorically and literally!"

The bell jingles behind her as the door closes.

Ayden sighs. "Remind me why you let her have keys to your place of business?"

"Because she'd break in anyway." I shrug.

He grins. "True."

The silence stretches for a beat — but it's a good kind of silence. Warm. Familiar.

I take a sip of my coffee and glance up at him. "So... a party?"

He smirks. "You heard the boss."

I roll my eyes, but I'm smiling. "You're actually going to let her plan this?"

"Let her? No one *lets* Beck do anything. She just decides it's happening."

I laugh, shaking my head. "You two are dangerous together."

"Admit it," he says, leaning closer across the counter, voice dropping. "You like dangerous."

My heart skips. "You're insufferable."

He grins. "You already said that."

I bump his shoulder, but he catches my hand before I can pull away, his thumb brushing softly over my knuckles. The teasing fades for a moment — replaced by that quiet, familiar heat that makes the world slow down.

"I like this," he says softly. "Us. Like this."

I smile. "Me too."

And even with Beck's chaos still lingering in the air, the bookstore feels peaceful again.

Maybe, for once, this story's finally starting to turn the page.

31
Serenity

If Beck says "trust me" one more time, I might actually combust.

"This is *not* what I agreed to," I mutter as I step into our apartment's living room.

The music's already thumping through the floorboards, the kind that makes your heartbeat sync to the bass. Colored lights flicker against the walls. Beck's draped fairy lights across the ceiling, and there's an actual *punch bowl,* because of course there is.

Beck twirls dramatically when she sees me. "See? It's cute!"

"Cute?" I gesture toward the doorway. "There are, like, forty people here, Beck."

"Correction," Luke says from the kitchen, already pouring drinks. "Forty-five."

I glare. "You invited half the campus?"

Beck grins, completely unbothered. "Word spread! You're popular, birthday girl. I take no responsibility."

Ayden walks in behind her, and the noise in my chest quiets just a little. He's wearing a dark shirt and jeans, hair still damp from his shower, sleeves rolled up. He looks unfairly good.

Beck notices the way my eyes linger and smirks. "Wow. You two cleaned up nicely. Look at you — all *romantic tension chic*."

Ayden groans. "Leave us alone."

She grins. "You love me."

"Questionable."

The night starts easy.

Music, laughter, drinks. The kind of chaos that feels harmless.

Beck somehow convinces Ayden to dance — or, more accurately, drags him into the middle of the room while everyone cheers. He looks ridiculous for about five seconds, then smirks and starts moving just enough to make everyone laugh.

Luke whoops. "Okay, Ayden's got moves!"

I laugh, clapping with everyone else. When his eyes find mine through the crowd, my smile falters — just slightly — because the way he's looking at me makes the whole room fade out.

It's comfortable for a while. Easy.

Until it isn't.

***

It starts small — just more people showing up. Then it grows like a weed.

Someone must've posted about the party, because within an hour, it's packed. I can barely move through the living room. There are students from the dorms, the basketball team, a few

179

people from my English class, even a couple of professors pretending they're not too old to be here.

Beck's in her element, laughing with Luke by the stereo. Ryan's handing out drinks. It's loud and messy, but it's fun — until I see *her*.

Ashley Kent.

Alix's best friend.

She's standing by the kitchen doorway, platinum hair shining under the string lights, red lipstick perfectly in place. The kind of girl who's never been uncomfortable a day in her life.

The second her eyes meet mine, that smug smile curves her lips.

I freeze.

Ayden sees her at almost the same time. His whole body goes tense.

Ashley takes a sip of her drink, tilts her head, and says loudly enough for half the room to hear, "Well, well. Serenity Evans."

The conversations nearby quiet just a little. People notice tension like they notice sparks — they turn toward it instinctively.

I force a polite smile. "Ashley."

She looks between me and Ayden, her expression feigning innocence. "Didn't expect to see you two so... cozy."

"Ashley," Ayden says flatly, stepping closer, "not tonight."

Her eyebrows lift. "Oh, come on. I'm just saying hi."

But her tone is too sweet — that kind of sugar that hides poison underneath.

"Though, I guess I shouldn't be surprised," she continues. "Considering how much you two used to argue about her."

The room stills just a little more.

I blink. "Excuse me?"

Ayden's voice hardens. "Ashley. Drop it."

She smiles — that same cold smile Alix used to wear when she wanted to hurt someone without raising her voice. "I mean, I heard all about it. The fights, the way she'd accuse you of being obsessed with Serenity. You never told her that part?"

My heart stops. "What are you talking about?"

Ayden's jaw clenches. "Ashley, I swear to God—"

"She was miserable that night," Ashley cuts in, her voice lower now, but everyone nearby can still hear. "Before she drove off. She said you were going to leave her for Serenity. That you already had."

The noise of the party fades completely.

All I can hear is my own pulse.

I look at Ayden — really look — and his face tells me everything before he even speaks.

He knew.

He's known.

"Ayden?" My voice cracks.

He tries to reach for me. "Serenity, please—"

"You knew," I whisper. "You knew she thought that. That she—" My throat tightens. "That she died thinking it was because of me."

"It wasn't like that," he says quickly. "She was upset, she wasn't thinking straight—"

"You should've told me."

"I wanted to," he says, desperate now. "I just—"

"Just what?" I snap. "Didn't want me to know the truth? That maybe I was part of what broke her?"

He shakes his head, stepping closer. "No. You weren't. You never were. Serenity, please—"

But I can't. I can't hear him. Because everything in my chest feels like it's collapsing inward.

The noise of the party creeps back in — laughter, music, someone yelling for more drinks — but it all feels far away.

Beck's voice cuts through it somewhere in the background, sharp and protective. "Ashley, get out."

But I'm already backing away.

Ayden reaches for me again, and I shake my head, tears burning behind my eyes. "You should've told me, Ayden."

"Serenity—"

"I trusted you."

The words break out of me before I can stop them. The air feels too tight. The walls too close.

I turn and push through the crowd, ignoring the way everyone parts around me, ignoring Beck calling after me, ignoring everything except the need to *breathe.*

Outside, the night air is cool and sharp. Fireworks crack somewhere in the distance — mocking, echoing, too much like last year.

I don't look back.

Not at the apartment.

Not at him.

Because I can't take hearing one more truth too late.

32

Serenity

The wind whips across my face, but I barely feel it. My chest hurts too much.

Ayden's voice catches behind me, breathless and pleading. "Serenity, please—just stop!"

I turn on him, shaking, tears streaking down my cheeks. "You should've told me, Ayden. You should've told me the truth a long time ago!"

"I know!" His voice breaks. "You're right, I should have. But you need to understand—"

"Understand what?" I snap. "That she died because of me? Because she thought you loved me?"

He steps forward, eyes burning with desperation. "It wasn't because of you. She made her own choice that night."

I shake my head. "You don't believe that."

"I do," he says, voice low and shaking. "Because I was there, Serenity. I was there until the second she left."

I freeze. "What do you mean?"

His jaw tightens. "We fought that night. About you."

My heart stops. "Ayden..."

"She said she could tell I cared about you. She was angry, jealous—hurt," he says, each word heavier than the last. "I tried to calm her down, but she wouldn't listen. She took my keys, got in the car, and sped off before I could stop her."

The world tilts around me. "You let her drive?"

"I didn't *let* her!" His voice cracks, pained. "By the time I realized what she was doing, she was already gone. I called her—God, I called her to explain, to tell her I was sorry, to tell her I never wanted to hurt her or you, but she—"

He stops, voice breaking apart.

"She what?" I whisper.

He swallows hard, eyes glassy. "She answered."

The silence between us stretches, suffocating.

"She was crying," he continues quietly. "And I was trying to tell her everything—how I felt, how none of it was supposed to happen like this. I told her I cared about you, Serenity, but not the way she thought. I just wanted her to understand that you didn't take anything from her."

He stops, trembling. "But she wouldn't listen. She just kept yelling. The last thing she said was—"

He swallows hard, like the words are poison.

"'Why her? Why my sister? Why Serenity?'"

My knees almost buckle.

His voice drops to a whisper. "Then I heard the crash."

The sound of it hangs between us — a memory neither of us was there to see, but both will carry forever.

"I called her name," he says, voice hoarse, breaking. "Over and over, but she didn't answer. I drove there as fast as I could, but it was already done."

Tears spill down my face faster than I can stop them. My hands are shaking. "You should've told me," I whisper. "You should've told me all of it."

"I wanted to," he says, his voice cracking. "But how was I supposed to tell you that your sister's last words were about you? That she died thinking you were the reason?"

I cover my mouth, a sob catching in my throat.

"She wasn't angry at you," he says, stepping closer, eyes wet. "She was angry at me. Because she was right. I loved you. I just didn't know it until it was too late."

The words rip through me like glass.

For a long time, we just stand there — two people who lost the same person, both broken by her in different ways. The wind picks up, scattering the sound of the party behind us into nothing.

Finally, I whisper, "You can't fix this, Ayden."

He nods slowly. "I know. But I can stop lying about it." He reaches for my hand, but before we make contact, I quickly move out of the way. Hurt flashes in his green eyes before he swallows and whispers, "I love you, Iris. I love you so much."

I shake my head, tears still falling. "You don't get to tell me you love me now. Not like this."

"I'm not saying it to make you forgive me," he says softly. "I'm saying it because it's the truth — and I can't keep living like it isn't."

I can't look at him anymore. The pain in his eyes mirrors my own, and it's too much.

So I turn away, my voice barely steady. "I need space."

He doesn't argue this time. Doesn't chase me.

"Okay," he says quietly. "Take all the time you need."

And as I walk away, I hear him whisper something to the wind — too soft to catch, but heavy enough to make me stop for half a second.

When I glance back, he's standing there under the streetlight, shoulders shaking, hands clenched like he's holding himself together by force.

For the first time, I don't see the boy who broke my heart.

I see the one who's been carrying his own all along.

33

Serenity

The bookstore is silent.

Too still, even for early morning. It feels like the whole building is holding its breath — the kind of quiet that doesn't soothe you, but presses down on your chest. I unlock the door anyway. Not because I want to be here, but because I can't stand being anywhere else.

Home feels too empty. My phone's full of unread messages. And the world outside keeps moving like it doesn't know everything in me just cracked.

So I came here — to the only place that's ever made sense.

I don't bother turning on the lights. The sun's already rising, bleeding gold through the big windows, painting stripes across the floorboards. The candles from last night are still half-melted on the tables. One of them flickers weakly when I walk past, as if it's still trying.

I drop my bag behind the counter and walk straight to the classics section — our section.

Mine and Ayden's.

The one we used to hide in when the world got too loud.

I sink to the floor, pulling my knees to my chest. The air smells like paper and dust and old cedar. My hand drifts along the shelf until my fingers brush against the spine of *To Kill a Mockingbird.*

The inside cover still has the same faint carving — *S.E. + A.J.* — barely visible now, but it's there.

Proof that we existed.

The tears come fast this time. Not the quiet, graceful kind. The ugly ones — the ones that burn your throat on the way out.

I'm sad.

God, I'm so sad.

But underneath it, deep below the surface is anger. Anger at Alix. Because she made me feel small my whole life.

Because she could ruin me with one word and then smile like nothing happened.

Because she's gone now, and I can't tell her how much that hurt.

She'd spend years reminding me that I'd never measure up, that I was the "sweet one," not the smart one, not the brave one.

And no matter how many times she humiliated me, I kept trying to make her love me anyway. Because that's what little sisters do — they keep reaching out, even when it burns.

And now she's gone, and I'm still trying to untangle the part of me that thought it was my fault.

Ashley's words from last night keep replaying —

"She said you were the reason."

"She said he loved you."

"She said—"

I squeeze my eyes shut. The memory is too loud.

Why her? Why my sister? Why Serenity?

That's how Alix went out — hating me.

And I can't forgive her for that. Not yet. Maybe not ever.

I hear the bell over the door chime softly.

I don't move.

Beck's footsteps echo softly on the floorboards. She finds me without asking, crouching down across from me, two coffees in hand. She looks like she hasn't slept — hair pulled back, makeup smudged, wearing one of Ayden's oversized sweatshirts.

She sets the cups down and sits beside me. "You look like hell."

I give a weak laugh. "You always know what to say."

She smiles sadly. "You wanna talk about it?"

"Not really," I whisper. "But I can't stop thinking about it anyway."

Beck nods, quiet for a long moment. "I'm sorry you had to find out like that. About that night."

"Yeah well," I say flatly. "Ashley made sure of that."

"Yeah." Beck sighs, rubbing her temple. "I wanted to drag her out by her hair."

I manage a tiny smile, but it fades fast. "She said Alix died thinking I was the reason Ayden didn't love her."

Beck looks at me carefully. "He told you what happened?"

I nod. "He said they fought. That she took his keys and left before he could stop her. That he called her to try to explain —

to tell her the truth — but she just kept yelling. The last thing she said was..." I swallow hard. "She asked him, 'Why her? Why my sister?' Then he heard the crash."

The words hang in the air between us, heavy and cruel.

Beck's eyes soften. "He's carried that with him every single day since."

"I know," I whisper. "But so have I. And I didn't even know I was carrying it."

We sit in silence for a moment, both staring at the floor.

Then Beck says quietly, "You're allowed to be mad at her."

I glance up, startled.

She shrugs. "Alix wasn't easy to love, Serenity. She could be cruel. You don't have to pretend she was perfect just because she's gone."

"I don't hate her," I say slowly. "I just... I'm mad that she got to leave me with all this. The guilt. The questions. The way she made me feel like I'd stolen something from her that I never even wanted."

Beck nods. "I know."

I laugh weakly, wiping my eyes. "She was supposed to be the strong one. The one who never fell apart. But she couldn't handle losing him."

"She couldn't handle herself," Beck says gently. "Ayden loved her, in his own way. But it wasn't enough. And she made it everyone else's fault."

Her voice catches. "Especially his."

I look down, twisting the paper sleeve of my coffee. "He should've told me."

"He thought he was protecting you."

"That's not protection, Beck. That's lying."

"I know."

The quiet stretches again. The hum of the city seeps through the window — cars passing, a bird somewhere on the ledge outside.

Finally, Beck says softly, "After the accident, he wasn't the same. He blamed himself so badly, I didn't think he'd make it through the semester. He quit basketball. Barely ate. Barely slept. I'd find him at the lake sometimes — the place she crashed near — just... sitting there. For hours."

My throat tightens. "He never told me that."

"He wouldn't," Beck says. "He didn't want you to see him broken."

"He was already broken."

Beck nods. "Yeah. So were you."

That hits harder than I expect. I blink back fresh tears.

She reaches out and squeezes my hand. "You're both still figuring it out. You don't have to forgive him yet. You don't even have to forgive her. But you've got to stop letting their ghosts talk louder than your own voice."

I stare at her, my chest tight. "What if I don't know what to say?"

"Then start with the truth," Beck says softly. "The one that hurts the most. Say it out loud so it stops owning you."

I take a shaky breath. The words sit heavy on my tongue.

"I'm mad at her," I whisper. "I miss her, but I'm so damn mad at her for leaving like that. For making me feel like I did something wrong. For making me hate myself just because Ayden saw me."

Beck squeezes my hand tighter. "Good. Say it."

"I hate that she's gone," I whisper, tears falling now. "I hate that she never gave me a chance to fix things. I hate that she made him feel like he had to choose."

The sob that comes next is sharp, tearing through the silence. Beck pulls me against her, holding me while I cry into her shoulder.

Neither of us says anything for a while. Just breathing. Just letting it all out.

When the tears finally stop, Beck sits back, brushing her thumb under my eye. "You needed that."

I nod weakly. "Yeah."

She smiles softly. "You know, he still loves you."

I close my eyes. "I don't know if that makes this better or worse."

"Maybe it's both," she says. "But it's real. And after everything, maybe that's the only thing that still matters."

I look around the bookstore — the flickering candlelight, the shelves lined with stories about people who fall and get back up again.
For the first time in what feels like forever, I can breathe.

"I forgive her," I say quietly. "But I don't forget."

Beck nods. "That's enough for today."

The sunlight catches the gold lettering on the spine of *The Great Gatsby,* and I think about the note Ayden left inside — *You're my green light at the end of the dock.*

For a long moment, I just stare at it, feeling the ache in my chest shift — not gone, not healed, but changing.

Maybe this is what forgiveness actually looks like.

Not letting go of the past — just learning to live with it.

34
Serenity

By afternoon the sky turns a dull gray, heavy and waiting. The words Beck left me with keep circling in my head — *You've got to stop letting their ghosts talk louder than your own voice.*

I close the bookstore early. The quiet doesn't help anymore. The air inside feels thick with memory, with things unsaid, with Alix.

Beck let me borrow her car for the day.

So I grab the keys and drive.

The road out of town winds past the lake and the hills. The clouds hang low enough to touch. Every mile feels heavier. I tell myself I'm just going to clear my head — but I already know where I'm headed.

By the time I reach the cemetery, the wind has picked up, carrying the faint smell of rain. The gate creaks when I push it open. The path is lined with wet leaves. Each step crunches underfoot, too loud in the stillness. I count them without meaning to, as if keeping rhythm will stop my thoughts from unraveling.

And then I see her name.

Alix Elizabeth Evans.

Clean letters, perfect stone, flowers starting to wilt.

My throat tightens.

I haven't been here since the funeral. Not because I didn't care — but because I didn't know what I'd say if I came.

Now I know exactly what I'd say.

Ten years earlier

We were thirteen and fifteen.

Alix had just gotten her first cheer uniform. She twirled in front of the mirror, shining and perfect, while I sat cross-legged on the bed with a book in my lap.

She turned suddenly. "Does this make me look older?"

I shrugged. "Maybe a little."

She frowned. "You don't know anything about fashion, Serenity. You're always wearing sweaters. You look like a librarian."

"I like sweaters," I said.

She rolled her eyes. "Of course you do. You like boring things. Books. Silence. People who don't exist."

I looked down at my knees. "They exist in stories."

"That's not the same." She leaned closer, lowering her voice. "You know what your problem is? You're scared to be seen. You hide behind all those nice-girl smiles and hope someone feels sorry for you."

"I don't—"

"Yes, you do." She straightened, satisfied. "You'll always be the quiet one. The one people forget."

Then she walked out, humming, leaving the smell of her new perfume behind like proof she'd been there.

Four Years Earlier

I was seventeen.

Ayden had just started staying over more often — the fights at his house were getting bad, and Dad didn't ask questions.

One night, Alix cornered me in the kitchen while he and Beck were asleep in the living room.

"You think he likes you?" she asked.

I froze, a glass of water halfway to my lips. "What?"

She smiled, all teeth. "You look at him like he hung the stars, Serenity. It's pathetic."

"That's not—"

"Don't lie," she said. "He's being nice to you because he feels bad for you. Because no one else does."

She reached out and tucked a strand of hair behind my ear — a sister's gesture that somehow felt like a threat. "You're sweet, but you're not special. Don't forget that."

I remember standing there long after she went to bed, the hum of the refrigerator filling the silence, trying to swallow down the lump in my throat.

present

The memories blur and fade as I crouch in front of her headstone.

For years I told myself she didn't mean it — that it was just sibling rivalry, that she was jealous or insecure.

But cruelty leaves fingerprints, and hers are still all over me.

I touch the top of the stone, cold and slick with dew. "You did everything you could to make me small," I whisper. "And it worked."

The words scrape my throat. "You called me weak. You made fun of everything I loved. You made me feel like being quiet was a flaw."

A tear falls onto the carved letters of her name. "And now you're gone, and I don't know how to hate you without feeling guilty."

The wind stirs through the grass, cool against my face.

"I know you were hurting," I say. "I know you thought everyone loved me more. But I never wanted to compete with you. I just wanted you to love me back."

My chest aches. "You didn't have to fight me for everything. You didn't have to die thinking I stole him from you. You already had everything I wanted—until you threw it away."

The first drop of rain lands on my hand. Then another.

"I'm angry, Alix. For what you said. For what you did. For how you left. But I'm also tired of carrying it."

The rain falls harder, washing down the stone, the flowers, my hands.

"I forgive you," I whisper, voice trembling. "But I'm not forgetting. Not anymore."

Thunder rumbles far off, and the clouds break just enough for a sliver of sunlight to cut through — pale and fleeting, lighting up her name.

For the first time, it doesn't hurt to look at it.

I stand slowly, brushing the wet grass from my jeans. "Wherever you are," I say softly, "I hope you've stopped fighting everything. I hope you found peace."

The breeze shifts, warm against my back, and I take it as the only answer I'll ever get.

As I walk back toward the gate, the rain begins to pour — cold, steady, cleansing.

I don't run.

I let it soak through my clothes, my hair, my skin, until I can't tell if the water on my face is rain or tears.

By the time I reach the car, the sky opens completely.

And for the first time since the night she died, I let myself breathe without feeling her shadow.

35
Serenity

The rain follows me all the way back into town. By the time I pull into the bookstore lot, it's more drizzle than storm, the kind of rain that clings instead of falls. The world smells like wet pavement and pine.

The lights are still on inside. I stop in the doorway for a second, confused. I don't remember leaving them on.

Then I see him.

Ayden's sitting on the floor behind the counter, back against the shelf where we used to read when we were kids. His legs are stretched out, a takeout cup balanced on his knee, his hoodie damp around the edges. He looks like he's been there a while.

For a moment, we just stare at each other.

"You're soaked," he says finally, his voice rough and low.

I close the door behind me, the bell chiming softly. "It's raining."

He gives a half-smile, faint and tired. "You're good at stating the obvious."

"Somebody has to be."

He stands, brushing off his hands like he's stalling for time. The movement's small, but I notice how restless he looks — how his fingers twitch like they're looking for something to hold.

"Why are you here?" I ask quietly.

"I didn't want to leave things the way they were."

"You mean broken?"

He exhales, running a hand through his hair. "I guess that's one word for it."

"You could've just called."

"I didn't think you'd answer." He's right. I probably wouldn't have.

The silence stretches between us—thick, heavy, and charged. The sound of the rain fills the space between words.

Finally, I whisper, "Beck told me what happened after Alix."

His eyes flick up fast. "She what?"

"She told me how bad it got. How you stopped showing up to practice. How you'd sit by the lake for hours."

He looks away, jaw tightening. "She had no right—"

"She had every right," I cut in, sharper than I mean to. "You've been carrying all of it alone. You didn't even let me see you break."

He flinches, and when he looks at me again, his expression softens. "I didn't want you to see me like that."

"You think I'd rather see you like *this*?" I whisper.

He doesn't answer. His silence says enough.

I walk closer until there's only a foot of space between us. The rain taps softly against the windows. "No more secrets, Ayden. I mean it this time."

He swallows hard, nodding once. "No more."

But something flickers in his eyes; a hesitation, a quiet panic that betrays him before he can mask it. It's there for only a second, but I catch it.

I see it.

And I know, even before he says anything else, that he's still hiding something.

Maybe not about Alix. Maybe something worse.

But I'm too tired to fight tonight.

So I do what I've done too many times before — I let it go.

Not because I don't care. Because I still love him enough to give him one more night before I start asking again.

He exhales, shoulders dropping, relief flickering across his face when I don't push. "Serenity," he says softly. "I'm sorry. For all of it. For what I said last year. For what I didn't say sooner."

My chest tightens. "You've already said you're sorry."

"I'll keep saying it until you believe it."

I shake my head. "That's not how it works."

He takes a step forward. "Then how does it?"

"By telling the truth when it's hard."

He looks down at the floor, then back up. "You already know the truth."

"No," I say gently. "I know the truth you're ready to tell."

The air shifts, heavier now. His eyes drop again, and his fingers twitch like they did before — like he's resisting the urge to reach for me and hide at the same time. Whatever it is he's not saying, it lives in the silence between us. I can feel it, humming just beneath his words.

Still, I step closer. "I forgive you," I whisper. "For everything you told me. But I can't forgive what I don't know. Not yet."

He looks up sharply, pain flashing across his face. "You're saying you don't trust me."

"I'm saying I want to."

That seems to undo him. His voice drops lower, quieter, like he's speaking more to himself than to me. "Then I'll try to be someone you can."

I nod. "Good."

We stand there for a long moment, the rain softening against the glass, our breath fogging the quiet between us. When he finally moves, it's slow — his hand brushing against mine, tentative, waiting for me to pull away.

I don't.

He exhales, relief and exhaustion bleeding together. His other hand comes up, brushing damp curls away from my face, fingertips tracing my jaw like he's memorizing me all over again.

"Serenity," he murmurs, and my name sounds like something sacred in his mouth.

Before I can answer, he leans down, and his lips meet mine.

It's not a desperate kiss — not like the ones born from anger and pain — but something quieter. Real. His hands cradle my face, his thumb tracing the edge of my cheekbone. I breathe him in — rain, coffee, the faint scent of cedar that always lingers on his clothes.

When he pulls back, he keeps his forehead pressed to mine. "I don't deserve this," he whispers.

"Maybe not," I say softly. "But you're still getting it."

He lets out a shaky laugh, half-relieved, half-afraid. "You always surprise me."

"Get used to it."

For a moment, we just stand there, holding each other while the rain slows outside. The bookstore is warm, quiet, familiar. It feels like we could stay like this forever — until I look up at him again.

He's smiling, but his eyes aren't at peace. There's something there — something guarded, flickering like a shadow behind the light.

I notice it. The way his jaw tightens when I look too long.

The way his gaze drifts toward the door, like something outside might come crashing through it at any second.

He catches me watching, and the smile returns — practiced, careful, the one he used to wear when he wanted me to stop asking questions.

And I do.

Not because I believe him.

But because I want this moment to last a little longer before it all unravels again.

He presses a soft kiss to my forehead and murmurs, "I love you."

I whisper it back, even though it feels heavy on my tongue.

When he pulls me closer, the quiet returns — warm, safe, and fleeting.

But even as I close my eyes, I know this peace is borrowed.

Because whatever Ayden's hiding hasn't gone away.

It's waiting.

And deep down, I can already feel it —

whatever's coming next will break us again.

36
Serenity

Friday night at the apartment feels almost normal again.

Beck has turned the living room into her version of a theater — twinkle lights draped across the curtain rods, every blanket we own piled on the couch, and a bowl of popcorn so large it looks like a dare.

Ryan and Luke are already camped out, bickering over what to watch. Ayden and I sit in the middle, a blanket shared between us, while Beck scrolls dramatically through streaming options like she's hosting an award show.

"Okay, my beautiful disasters," Beck says, pointing the remote like a wand. "Choose your fighter: rom-com, action, or horror."

"No horror," Ayden says immediately.

"Of course not," Luke teases. "Wouldn't want you crying in front of your girlfriend."

Ryan leans into him. "I think it's sweet. Look at them, all cuddled up. You'd never know Mr. Broody Basketball Star here used to hiss at emotions."

Beck gasps, clutching her chest. "Excuse me? I worked *hard* to fix that. I deserve producer credit for this entire relationship."

Ayden groans. "Beck—"

She cuts him off. "Don't you *Beck* me. You asked for my help, remember? Operation Don't-Let-Ayden-Die-Alone was my idea."

My head snaps toward her. "Wait, what?"

Ryan smirks. "Oh, she didn't tell you? We all knew. The book-store setup, the candles, the note — total team effort."

Luke grins. "Beck had spreadsheets."

"Spreadsheets?" I echo, the horror laced in my voice.

Beck waves a hand. "Creative direction requires planning. You can't just wing a confession like that."

Ayden drops his head back against the couch. "I can't believe you told them."

"Please," she says, popping a piece of popcorn in her mouth. "You two were my magnum opus. If I don't brag, who will?"

Ryan raises his drink. "To Beck, patron saint of meddling."

Luke clinks his glass against his. "And to the lovebirds who finally got their act together."

Ayden groans again. "I hate you all."

"No, you don't," Beck sing-songs. "You love me. I'm your emotional GPS."

"More like a traffic jam," he mutters.

The laughter that follows fills the whole room — easy, bright, and genuine.

For a while, we forget everything heavy. The movie starts a rom-com Beck insisted on), and soon Ryan and Luke are whispering inside jokes, Beck's quoting the dialogue before the characters can, and Ayden's arm drapes over my shoulders.

Halfway through, Beck pauses the screen mid–love confession and points at us.

"Look at them," she says. "They're the same level of disgustingly adorable. It's like watching a live-action sequel."

Ayden raises an eyebrow. "You're never going to stop talking about this, are you?"

"Not when I spent *weeks* helping you rehearse your lines."

He smirks. "Lines? You make it sound scripted."

Beck winks. "Please. I wrote half of them."

Everyone bursts out laughing, and before I can say a word, Ayden shakes his head, grinning. "You want proof it wasn't scripted?" He turns to me and kisses me.

It's not long or showy, just quiet and sure, but the room immediately erupts.

Beck throws popcorn in the air. Ryan claps. Luke whistles.

"Finally!" Beck yells. "A live encore performance!"

Ryan grins. "Romantic *and* brave. Ten out of ten."

Luke nods. "Could've used more dramatic lighting, but solid work overall."

Ayden pulls back, smiling against my forehead. "Happy now?"

"Ecstatic," Beck says. "I can die fulfilled."

I hide my face in the blanket. "You're all impossible."

"And we love you too," Ryan teases.

The laughter keeps going, fading only when the movie starts again. I lean into Ayden's side, his hand resting over mine un-

208

der the blanket. He smells faintly like rain and coffee, warmth grounding me.

For a while, it feels like we're untouchable — like maybe everything that's happened is finally behind us.

But when the credits roll and the others start packing up to leave, Beck glances at her phone and frowns. "Hey, did you guys see this?"

She turns the screen toward me. It's a social media post — bright lettering over a photo of the Green Haven campus quad lit up with candles.

Iota Zeta Nu Memorial Bash—Celebrating the Life of Alix Evans. One Year Later. Saturday Night.

My stomach twists immediately.

Ryan leans over Beck's shoulder. "They're doing another one of those?"

Luke nods. "Her old sorority's been planning it for weeks."

Beck's voice softens. "You okay, Ren?"

I stare at the image — the same smile of Alix that used to hang in our hallway, all perfect edges and practiced warmth. "Yeah," I say automatically, though it sounds like a lie even to me.

Ayden's hand finds mine. "You don't have to go."

"I know."

But the truth is, part of me already knows I will.

Something about it feels wrong — too loud, too public, too *perfect.* Alix hated vulnerability. She lived for appearances. The idea of a party in her name, a celebration built on smiles and champagne, feels like another mask she left behind.

A bad feeling settles in my chest — heavy and instinctive. Like a warning.

Beck notices but doesn't press. "We'll talk about it tomorrow, okay?"

I nod. "Yeah."

After everyone leaves and the apartment goes quiet, I catch Ayden watching me again — the smile gone, something unreadable in his eyes. His phone buzzes once on the table, a message he turns facedown without reading.

I pretend not to notice.

But that uneasy feeling doesn't fade.

Not about the message.

Not about the party.

Just before I turn off the lights, I glance at the photo still open on my phone; my sister's smiling face frozen in time—and the caption beneath it:

Let's make this a night Alix would be proud of.

Somehow, I already know she would be.

And deep down, I know the night won't end the way anyone expects.

37
Serenity

The world feels wrong before I even step through the door.

The music inside the Iota Zeta Nu house is pounding, flashing lights cutting through the haze, laughter blurring into something too loud to be real. It smells like perfume and alcohol and the past I've spent a year trying to bury.

The moment I walk in, it's like I'm back in time — back to that first night when the world cracked open. The same song. The same laughter. The same ghosts.

I push through the crowd, the music vibrating in my ribs, the air too thick to breathe. Every face is a blur, every sound too sharp. Somewhere above the noise, I hear Alix's name shouted, her memory toasted like a brand, and it makes me sick.

Because they didn't know her. Not like I did.

They didn't know how cruel she could be when the music stopped.

They didn't know what it was like to live in her shadow and still ache for her light.

I swallow hard and force myself to keep moving.

Ayden's somewhere in the living room, Beck beside him, laughing too loudly at something Luke said. He looks up, catches my eye, smiles like he's relieved. I look away before the expression can reach me.

I need air.

I find it in the kitchen, but the silence there isn't better. That's where Ashley finds me.

She looks too perfect for a night built on ghosts — hair curled, makeup flawless, smile rehearsed. The same as before.

"Serenity," she says, voice honeyed and soft. "Can we talk? Just for a minute?"

Every instinct tells me no, but I nod anyway.

She lowers her voice. "I wanted to apologize. For last week. I shouldn't have said what I did about Ayden and Alix. It was cruel."

I cross my arms. "You think?"

"I mean it," she insists. "I was angry, and I took it out on you. You didn't deserve it."

There's a pause. I can almost believe her — until she exhales and says, "But I think you deserve the truth since Ayden refuses to tell you."

I feel sick to my stomach at her words. "What truth?"

She looks down, feigning hesitation, then meets my eyes. "Alix told me. Before she died. She said you were adopted."

The words don't make sense at first.

"What?"

"She said she found papers in your father's office. She said you never knew."

I stare at her, waiting for her to take it back. "You're lying."

Ashley shakes her head slowly. "I wish I was."

The air leaves my lungs. The sound of the party fades to a distant echo.

My legs move before my mind catches up. I don't remember leaving the kitchen. I don't remember running into the street. Only the rain hitting my skin and the cold in my throat as I gasp for air.

By the time I reach Sunshine Books, I'm drenched. The windows are dark, the sign in the door new.

PERMANENTLY CLOSED.

The words stare back at me, bold and final.

I press my hand against the glass, heart hammering. The store that raised me. The walls that knew every version of me. Gone.

My reflection wavers in the rain — a stranger's face looking back.

Something in me cracks open. I run again.

My parents' house is a blur of light and shadow, the porch light cutting through the storm. I pound on the door until it opens.

My father's face appears — sharp, tired, irritated. "Serenity. What are you doing here?"

"Tell me it's not true," I gasp. "Tell me you didn't sell the bookstore."

He scoffs. "Of course I did. It's been bleeding money for years."

"You didn't even tell me!"

"You don't own it," he snaps. "It was mine to sell."

"Why?" My voice shakes. "Why now?"

He leans against the frame, lips curling. "Because the offer was too good. And if you want to thank someone for keeping you distracted while I signed the papers—thank Ayden."

My stomach drops. "What?"

He smirks, cruel and casual. "He's been keeping you busy for weeks. That boy knows which side to play on. Your little boyfriend made sure you stayed out of the way."

I stumble back. "You're lying."

He shrugs. "Believe what you want, but Sunshine Books is gone. It's business, Serenity. Grow up."

And then he shuts the door in my face.

I didn't have the heart ask him about me being adopted.

The world blurs again. The rain pounds harder, washing everything into streaks of silver and black. I can't feel my hands. My chest feels hollow.

By the time I reach the Iota house again, I'm shaking — from the cold, from the anger, from the truth clawing its way out of me.

38

Serenity

Iris- The Goo Goo Dolls

The rain hasn't stopped since the moment I left the house.

The streets blur under the neon lights, puddles swallowing the reflections of cars that rush past, the storm swallowing everything else. My hair sticks to my skin, my lungs burn, but I keep running anyway—back to the party, back to the noise, back to him.

When I reach the Iota Zeta Nu house, the music is still pulsing. The laughter and voices, the same perfume and haze—it's all a ghost of that night a year ago. I can almost hear her laugh through it, the same cruel sweetness that used to cut right through me.

I push through the door, soaked, shaking, dizzy. The smell of cheap liquor and roses wraps around me like a memory I can't claw out of.

And then I see him.

Ayden.

He's standing near the bar with Beck, Luke, and Ryan. They're laughing, but the second his eyes find mine, the sound dies. His smile fades. The whole room seems to still.

"Serenity?" he says, his voice soft, worried.

"Iris."

He freezes. That one word—the one that always meant *stop*, the one that always meant *enough*—shatters the air between us.

He moves toward me, slow, cautious. "What happened?"

My hands shake at my sides. I can't tell if it's from the cold or the truth that's clawing up my throat.

"I found out," I say, my voice raw. "Ashley told me. That Alix told her I'm adopted."

His expression falters, eyes darkening. "Who told you?"

"I said Ashley," I bite out, my chest tightening. "But it doesn't matter. What matters is that *you knew*. You knew, Ayden, and you didn't tell me."

He takes a breath, the muscles in his jaw tense. "It wasn't my place—"

"Don't you dare," I snap. "Don't tell me it wasn't your place. You promised me no more secrets. You looked me in the eyes and said that. You let me stand there believing you, and this whole time—"

"Serenity, please—"

"You lied," I whisper. "Again."

The noise around us has gone quiet, like even the music knows it isn't welcome here. Beck's face is pale in the corner of my eye, Luke's hand resting on her shoulder to keep her back.

Ayden reaches for me, but I take a step away.

"And that's not even the worst part," I say, my voice breaking. "My dad sold the bookstore."

His eyes widen. "He what?"

"It's gone, Ayden." I can barely get the words out. "The sign's already up. Permanently closed. And do you know what he said when I showed up at his door? He said I could thank you for keeping me distracted while he made the deal."

He shakes his head, panic flooding his features. "No. That's not true. I didn't know—"

"But you didn't *stop* it, did you?" I say, my voice cracking. "You were with me every day, Ayden. Every single day. You knew he was planning something. You knew, and you still—"

"I was trying to protect you!" he yells, his voice breaking, his eyes desperate. "Everything I did was to protect you."

I laugh, the sound hollow and sharp. "No. Everything you did was to protect yourself. From me. From the truth."

He takes another step toward me, but I don't move this time. I want to hear it—I want to see his face when he realizes I finally see him for who he is.

"You think I didn't want to tell you?" he says, his voice low, trembling. "You think it didn't kill me to keep it from you? I knew, Serenity. I knew, and I didn't tell you because I thought it would destroy you."

"You don't get to make that decision for me." My voice is shaking so hard I can barely form the words. "You don't get to choose which truths I can survive."

He looks at me, broken. "I never meant to hurt you."

"But you did," I whisper. "Over and over."

I can feel the tears finally fall—hot against the cold rain still dripping from my hair. "You were supposed to be the one person who didn't lie to me. The one person who stayed. But all you ever do is leave me with half truths."

His voice cracks when he says my name again. "Ren—"

"No," I whisper. "Don't."

I take a step back, and his hand falls uselessly to his side.

"I don't even know who you are anymore."

"You do," he says weakly. "You know me better than anyone."

I shake my head, the words catching in my throat. "I used to."

For a heartbeat, neither of us moves. The music picks up again in the background, laughter rising from another room, but it sounds far away, like it belongs to another world.

I take one last look at him—the boy who once made me feel like I was more than my shadows—and realize he's the reason they grew darker.

And then I turn away.

He calls after me, his voice cracking like glass. "Serenity, please!"

But I keep walking. Out the door. Down the steps. Into the storm.

The rain hits harder this time, cold enough to sting, heavy enough to hide the tears that won't stop falling. My shoes slap against the pavement, the sound drowned out by thunder. I don't stop. I can't.

The night folds around me, the world reduced to rain and heartbreak and the weight of everything I've lost.

Sunshine Books. My family. Him. Myself.

All of it gone.

I walk until I can't see the house anymore. Until I can't hear the music. Until it's just me and the storm.

And somewhere between the flashes of lightning and the gasps for air, it hits me—the truth I've been running from all this time.

That maybe this was always how it was supposed to end. Maybe the world was never meant to stay kind to people like me—people who keep trying to fix what's already shattered.

I keep walking, the rain washing everything away, until the light from the Iota house disappears completely behind me.

39

Ayden

Chicago glows in the distance, all steel and light, a city pretending not to notice how broken it really is. I'm parked in front of my father's office, staring up at the windows that look like cold, watching eyes.

I came here to end it — to tell him I'm done with his deals, his control, his way of poisoning everything I touch.

But my hands won't stop shaking.

Every time I blink, I see Serenity's face.

The way she looked at me before she walked away.

"*I don't even know who you are anymore.*"

The words echo in my head until they sound like my own voice. My phone vibrates in my lap, screen lighting up in the dark. *Beck.*

I answer immediately. "Beck? I'm about to—"

Her voice cracks, high and terrified. "Ayden—It's Mom."

Something in my chest seizes. "What about her?"

"She—she's not breathing right," she stammers. "The doctors said the infection spread too fast. She's in septic shock—Ayden, they said she's dying!"

My heart stops. The sound that leaves my throat isn't a word. It's just air.

"I'm coming," I say, already flooring the gas.

***

The road to the rehab center is a blur of rain and panic.

I can barely see, but I don't slow down. My headlights carve through the storm, slicing the dark into brief flashes of gold and gray.

All I can hear is Beck's voice, breaking over the phone.

"They said she's dying."

And beneath that—my father's voice, cruel and distant: *"You think the world owes you something, boy? The only thing you'll ever inherit is the mess you make."*

He was wrong.

I inherited *his.*

I should have stopped him years ago.

When I was ten, I heard the first slap.

When I was twelve, Mom started hiding bruises under her sleeves.

When I was sixteen and he started taking it out on me instead, and she begged me not to fight back because "he'll only make it worse."

I let her protect me.

I let her take the hits, the blame, the silence.

And I told myself I was keeping her safe by surviving.

Now she's dying because I kept surviving.

***

By the time I reach the rehab center, the rain has slowed to a whisper.

The fluorescent lights inside sting my eyes. Beck's in the waiting room, her hoodie soaked, mascara smeared down her cheeks. She looks up the moment I walk in, and I can see it; the helplessness, the exhaustion, the fear.

"They won't let us in," she chokes out. "They're trying to make her comfortable."

"Comfortable?" My voice cracks. "She's dying, Beck. There's no comfort in that."

She doesn't answer. She just folds in on herself, her shoulders shaking. When the doctor finally walks out, I already know. His face says everything.

"Your mother is in multiple organ failure," he tells us gently. "The infection progressed faster than expected. We've done everything we can."

Beck's sob is instant. Loud. Shattering.

I just stand there, numb.

"You can go in now," the doctor says softly.

The room smells like antiseptic soap. The machines hum low and steady, indifferent to the chaos they're measuring. Mom lies motionless under the thin white sheets, smaller than I remember.

Beck rushes to her side, gripping her hand. "She's still warm," she whispers. "She's still here."

But she isn't. Not really.

I move closer, every step heavier than the last, until I'm beside the bed. I sit down, stare at her face — pale, fragile, still.

"Mom," I whisper, my voice trembling. "It's me. I'm here."

Beck's sobs fill the room. I can't look at her.

I can't look at anything but Mom.

Her hand is cold now.

I brush my thumb across her knuckles, the same way she used to do for me when I couldn't sleep after one of Dad's outbursts. "You were supposed to make it," I whisper. "You promised." Beck's breath hitches beside me, but I can't stop.

"I was going to tell him tonight," I say quietly. "I was going to tell him I was done—that I wasn't going to let him ruin us anymore."

Beck looks at me through her tears. "She would've been proud."

I shake my head. "No. She would've told me I should've done it years ago."

The beeping slows.

I press my forehead against her hand. "I'm sorry," I choke out. "For not stopping him. For not protecting you. For letting him turn me into him."

The beeping slows even more.

Beck starts sobbing harder, begging for the doctors, but they already know.

The sound of flatlines begin—and my heart dies along with my mother.

Beck's scream cuts through the room, splitting the air in two. Nurses rush in, their faces blurred by tears and light, but I don't move.

I just stare at Mom's hand in mine, waiting for it to warm again. Waiting for her to tell me it's not my fault.

But she doesn't.

Because it is my fault.

***

I don't remember walking out. Just the rain. Just the quiet that follows after the noise.

Beck's asleep in the passenger seat when I finally start driving. Her face is pressed against the window, her mouth parted slightly. She looks younger like this. Softer. I take her back to the apartment, placing her on the couch, covering her sleeping body with a blanket. I don't want to leave her alone, but if I don't go for a drive or do something, I will fucking lose it. I lightly lock up our apartment door before getting back into my car.

I grip the steering wheel until my fingers ache. The road stretches out in front of me, dark and endless. Every sound feels too loud. The silence feels worse.

I can't stop thinking—If I'd told Serenity sooner.

If I'd told my father to burn in hell years ago.

If I'd taken Mom and Beck and left.

If I'd been brave.

She might still be alive. Serenity might still love me.

But I didn't. And now everything I love is gone.

I pull over on the side of the highway. The city's lights blur through the rain, streaking down the windshield like tears I can't hold back.

I rest my forehead against the steering wheel, breathing in shallow, broken gasps until it all spills out.

The scream rips out of me before I can stop it — raw, empty, the kind of sound that doesn't make you feel better, only emptier. I scream until my throat feels completely raw.

Then the silence comes. Heavier than before.

And it hits me — all at once — like the truth has been waiting to crush me until I stopped fighting it.

I could have stopped all of this.

All of it. If I had stood up to my father sooner. If I hadn't let fear chain me to his shadow. If I hadn't let the guilt rot me from the inside out.

It's eating me alive.

Every breath. Every thought. Every heartbeat.

Because it wasn't just Mom I couldn't save. It was everyone.

Serenity. Beck. Myself.

The rain keeps falling, tracing patterns across the windshield, blurring the world into light and shadow.

And as I sit there, thoughts of how things ended up like this form in my head— slow, heavy, and final.

The hopeless and never-ending journey of a soul trying to remember the reason why it was put on this earth to begin with; it's hard to see the light when you're drowning in the shadows, trying to hold onto something—anything—but by the time you catch your breath and feel your lungs gasping for air, the darkness has a way of pulling you back under. And by then, the only thing that's left is the quiet and harrowing reminder that not only are you alone, but it was your own doing that made this nightmare become a reality.

THE END.

Acknowledgements

When I got the idea for this book two years ago, it started as an escape from my own reality. Like Serenity, I also struggle with skin conditions; Hidradenitis Suppurativa, Eczema, and Psoriasis. Writing this book has made me so proud to shed light on the struggles of living with skin conditions; especially Hidradenitis Suppurativa. I can honestly say I have never read a book that sheds light on this condition, and I wanted to write something that I wish I could have read in the worser times of this condition for me. Throughout the years of writing this book, Serenity and Ayden's story developed into something so dear and close to my heart. Thank you for taking the time to read their story.

To my readers:

Thank you so much for taking a piece of your time to read my debut novel. I hope you all fell in love with these characters and their story as I did, and my ultimate hope is that if you're struggling with anything similar to what these characters have gone through and will go through in the future, that it helps you feel seen and heard; less alone. Tangled Pages is not just a romance story; it's so much more.

To my parents and family:

Thank you for constantly believing in me. Thank you for constantly pushing me to achieve my dreams. I never thought I would actually finish this book and I truly have you all to thank for it. Thank you for always being my number one supporters since the day I was born. I love you!

To my friends:

Thank you for supporting me and listening to me babble on and on about this story for months. Your support means the world to me; more than you'll ever know.

To Serenity and Ayden:

Hi, my book babies. Writing this first part of your story will forever be the highlight of my life. I'm honored that I got to tell your story and share it with the world. I'm excited to continue writing your journey over the next two books. Thank you for letting me find ways to heal with the broken parts of me through writing your story. You two have helped heal in ways you'll never know. Thank you for taking over my heart and soul for the last two years. I can't wait to see how tangled your stories will remain over the next two books.

Bye for now.

I'll see you in the next Tangled Pages.

Socials

Feel free to follow me on my socials to stay updated on the latest news and updates on the Tangled Series!

instagram.com/

tiktok.com/@writtenbytrin_?_t=ZP-90qYQkp6NfL&_r=1

About the author

Trinity Elise is an African-American author from Illinois. She loves heart-breaking love stories; especially the forbidden ones. When she isn't reading a book, she makes a hobby out of watching the Scream movies on repeat and spending time with friends and family.